THE MOUSE AND THE MOTORCYCLE

Enjoy all of BEVERLY CLEARY'S books

FEATURING RAMONA QUIMBY:

Beezus and Ramona
Ramona the Pest
Ramona the Brave
Ramona and Her Father
Ramona and Her Mother
Ramona Quimby, Age 8
Ramona Forever
Ramona's World

••••

FEATURING HENRY HUGGINS:

Henry Huggins
Henry and Beezus
Henry and Ribsy
Henry and the Paper Route
Henry and the Clubhouse
Ribsy

••••

FEATURING RALPH MOUSE:

The Mouse
and the Motorcycle
Runaway Ralph
Ralph S. Mouse

MORE GREAT FICTION BY BEVERLY CLEARY:

Ellen Tebbits
Otis Spofford
Fifteen
The Luckiest Girl
Jean and Johnny
Emily's Runaway
Imagination
Sister of the Bride
Mitch and Amy
Socks
Dear Mr. Henshaw
Muggie Maggie
Strider
Two Times the Fun

••••

AND DON'T MISS BEVERLY CLEARY'S AUTOBIOGRAPHIES:

A Girl from Yamhill
My Own Two Feet

BEVERLY CLEARY

THE MOUSE AND THE MOTORCYCLE

ILLUSTRATED BY
JACQUELINE ROGERS

HARPER

An Imprint of HarperCollins*Publishers*

Library of Congress Catalog Card Number: 2013940666

ISBN 978-0-06-265798-5

Typography by Sarah Nichole Kaufman

21   PC/LSCH   10 9 8 7 6 5 4 3

Harper Classic edition, 2017

CONTENTS

1

THE NEW GUESTS

Keith, the boy in the rumpled shorts and shirt, did not know he was being watched as he entered Room 215 of the Mountain View Inn. Neither did his mother and father, who both looked hot and tired. They had come from Ohio and for five days had driven across plains and deserts and over mountains to the old hotel in the California foothills twenty-five miles from Highway 40.

The fourth person entering Room 215 may have known he was being watched, but he did not care. He was Matt, sixty if he was a day, who at the moment was the bellboy. Matt also replaced worn-out light-bulbs, renewed washers in leaky faucets, carried trays for people who telephoned room service to order food sent to their rooms, and sometimes prevented children from hitting one another with croquet mallets on the lawn behind the hotel.

Now Matt's right shoulder sagged with the weight of one of the bags he was carrying. "Here you are, Mr. Gridley. Rooms 215 and 216," he said, setting the smaller of the bags on a luggage rack at the foot of the double bed before he opened a door into the next room. "I expect you and Mrs. Gridley will want Room 216. It is a corner room with twin beds and a private bath." He carried the heavy bag into the next room, where he could be heard opening windows. Outside a chipmunk chattered in a pine tree and a chickadee whistled *fee-bee-bee*.

The boy's mother looked critically around Room 215 and whispered, "I think we should drive back to the main highway. There must be a motel with a *Vacancy* sign someplace. We didn't look long enough."

"Not another mile," answered the father. "I'm not driving another mile on a California highway on a holiday weekend. Did you see the way that truck almost forced us off the road?"

"Dad, did you see those two fellows on motorcycles—" began the boy and stopped, realizing he should not interrupt an argument.

"But this place is so *old*," protested the boy's mother. "And we have only three weeks for our whole trip. We had planned to spend the Fourth of July weekend in San Francisco and we wanted to show Keith as much of the United States as we could."

"San Francisco will have to wait, and this is part of the United States. Besides, this used to be a very fashionable hotel," said Mr. Gridley. "People came from miles around."

"Fifty years ago," said Mrs. Gridley. "And they came by horse and buggy."

4

The bellboy returned to Room 215. "The dining room opens at six-thirty, sir. There is Ping-Pong in the game room, TV in the lobby, and croquet on the back lawn. I'm sure you will be very comfortable." Matt, who had seen guests come and go for many years, knew there were two kinds—those who thought the hotel was a dreadful old barn of a place and those who thought it charming and quaint, so quiet and restful.

"Of course we will be comfortable," said Mr. Gridley, dropping some coins into Matt's hand for carrying the bags.

"But this big old hotel is positively spooky." Mrs. Gridley made one last protest. "It is probably full of mice."

Matt opened the window wide. "Mice? Oh no, ma'am. The management wouldn't stand for mice."

"I wouldn't mind a few mice," the boy said, as he looked around the room at the high ceiling, the knotty pine walls, the carpet so threadbare that many of its roses had almost entirely faded, the one chair with the antimacassar on its back, the washbasin and towel racks in the corner of the room. "I like it here," he announced. "A whole room to myself. Usually I just get a cot in the corner of a motel room."

His mother smiled, relenting. Then she turned to Matt. "I'm sorry. It's just that it was so hot crossing Nevada and we are not used to mountain driving. Back on the highway the traffic was bumper to bumper. I'm sure we shall be very comfortable."

After Matt had gone, closing the door behind him, Mr. Gridley said, "I need a rest before dinner. Four hundred miles of driving and that mountain traffic! It was too much."

"And if we are going to stay for a weekend I had better unpack," said Mrs. Gridley. "At least I'll have a chance to do some drip-drying."

Alone in Room 215 and unaware that he was being watched, the boy began to explore. He got down on his hands and knees and looked under the bed. He leaned out the open window as far as he could and greedily inhaled deep breaths of pine-scented air. He turned the hot and cold water on and off in the washbasin and slipped one of the small bars of paper-wrapped soap into his pocket. Under the window he discovered a knothole in the pine wall down by the floor and, squatting, poked his finger into the hole. When he felt nothing inside he lost interest.

Next Keith opened his suitcase and took out an apple and several small cars—a sedan, a sports car, and an ambulance about six inches long, and a red motorcycle half the length of the cars—which he dropped on the striped bedspread before he bit into the apple. He ate the apple noisily in big chomping bites, and then laid the core on the bedside table between the lamp and the telephone.

Keith began to play, running his cars up and down the bedspread, pretending that the stripes on the spread were highways and making noises with his mouth—*vroom vroom* for the sports car, *wh-e-e wh-e-e* for the ambulance, and *pb-pb-b-b-b* for the motorcycle, up and down the stripes.

Once Keith stopped suddenly and looked quickly around the room as if he expected to see something or someone, but when he saw nothing unusual he returned to his cars. *Vroom vroom. Bang! Crash!* The sports car hit the sedan and rolled over off the highway stripe. *Pb-pb-b-b-b.* The motorcycle came roaring to the scene of the crash.

"Keith," his mother called from the next room. "Time to get washed for dinner."

"OK." Keith parked his cars in a straight line on the bedside table beside the

telephone, where they looked like a row of real cars only much, much smaller.

The first thing Mrs. Gridley noticed when she and Mr. Gridley came into the room was the apple core on the table. She dropped it with a thunk into the metal wastebasket beside the table as she gave several quick little sniffs of the air and said, looking perplexed, "I don't care what the bellboy said. I'm sure this hotel has mice."

"I hope so," muttered Keith.

2

THE MOTORCYCLE

Except for one terrifying moment when the boy had poked his finger through the mousehole, a hungry young mouse named Ralph eagerly watched everything that went on in Room 215. At first he was disappointed at the size of the boy who was to occupy the room. A little child, preferably two or even three children, would have been better. Little messy children were always considerate about leaving crumbs on the carpet. Oh well, at least these people did not have a dog. If there was one thing Ralph disliked, it was a snoopy dog.

Next Ralph felt hopeful. Medium-sized boys could almost always be counted on to leave a sticky candy bar wrapper on the floor or a bag of peanuts on the bedside table, where Ralph could reach them by climbing up the telephone cord. With a boy this size, the food, though not apt to be plentiful, was almost sure to be of good quality.

The third emotion felt by Ralph was joy when the boy laid the apple core by the telephone. This was followed by despair when the mother dropped the core into the metal wastebasket. Ralph knew that anything at the bottom of a metal wastebasket was lost to a mouse forever.

A mouse lives not by crumbs alone and so Ralph experienced still another emotion;

this time food was not the cause of it. Ralph was eager, excited, curious, and impatient all at once. The emotion was so strong it made him forget his empty stomach. It was caused by those little cars, especially that motorcycle and the *pb-pb-b-b-b* sound the boy made. That sound seemed to satisfy something within Ralph, as if he had been waiting all his life to hear it.

Pb-pb-b-b-b went the boy. To the mouse the sound spoke of highways and speed, of distance and danger, and whiskers blown back by the wind.

The instant the family left the room to go to dinner, Ralph scurried out of the mouse-hole and across the threadbare carpet to the telephone cord, which came out of a hole in the floor beside the bedside table.

"Ralph!" scolded his mother from the mousehole. "You stay away from that telephone cord!" Ralph's mother was a great worrier. She worried because their hotel was old and run-down and because so many rooms were often empty with no careless guests to leave crumbs behind for mice. She worried about the rumor that their hotel was to be torn down when the new highway came through. She worried about her children finding aspirin tablets. Ralph's father had tried to carry an aspirin tablet in his cheek pouch, the aspirin had dissolved with unexpected suddenness, and Ralph's father had been poisoned. Since then no member of the family would think of touching an aspirin tablet, but this did not prevent Ralph's mother from worrying.

Most of all Ralph's mother worried about Ralph. She worried because he was a reckless mouse, who stayed out late in the daytime when he should have been home safe in bed. She worried when Ralph climbed the curtain to sit on the windowsill to watch the chipmunk in the pine tree outside and the cars in the parking lot below. She worried because Ralph wanted to go exploring down the hall instead of traveling under the floorboards like a sensible mouse. Heaven only knew what dangers he might meet in the hall—maids, bellboys, perhaps even cats. Or what was worse, vacuum cleaners. Ralph's mother had a horror of vacuum cleaners.

Ralph, who was used to his mother's worries, got a good running start and was already halfway up the telephone cord.

"Remember your Uncle Victor!" his mother called after him.

Ralph seemed not to hear. He climbed the cord up to the telephone, jumped down, and ran around to the row of cars. There it was on the end—the motorcycle! Ralph stared at it and then walked over and kicked a tire. Close up the motorcycle looked even better than he expected. It was new and shiny and had a good set of tires. Ralph walked all the way around it, examining the pair of chromium mufflers and the engine and the hand clutch. It even had a little license plate so it would be legal to ride it.

"Boy!" said Ralph to himself, his whiskers quivering with excitement. "Boy, oh, boy!" Feeling that this was an important moment in his life, he took hold of the handgrips. They felt good and solid beneath his paws. Yes, this motorcycle was a good machine all right. He could tell by the feel. Ralph threw a leg over the motorcycle and sat jauntily on the plastic seat. He even bounced up and down. The seat was curved just right to fit a mouse.

But how to start the motorcycle? Ralph did not know. And even if he did know how to start it, he could not do much riding up here on the bedside table. He considered pushing the motorcycle off onto the floor, but he did not want to risk damaging such a valuable machine.

Ralph bounced up and down on the seat a couple more times and looked around for some way to start the motorcycle. He pulled at a lever or two but nothing happened. Then a terrible thought spoiled his pleasure. This was only a toy. It would not run at all.

Ralph, who had watched many children in Room 215, had picked up a lot of information about toys. He had seen a boy from Cedar Rapids throw his model airplane on the floor because he could not make its plastic parts fit properly. A little girl had burst into tears and run sobbing to her mother when her doll's arm had come out of its socket. And then there was that nice boy, the potato chip nibbler, who stamped his foot because the batteries kept falling out of his car.

But this toy could not be like all those other toys he had seen. It looked too perfect with its wire spokes in its wheels and its pair of shiny chromium exhaust pipes. It would not be right if it did not run. It would not be *fair*. A motorcycle that looked as real as this one *had* to run. The secret of making it run must be perfectly simple if only Ralph had someone to show him what it was.

Ralph was not satisfied just sitting on the motorcycle. Ralph craved action. After all, what was a motorcycle for if it wasn't action? Who needed motorcycle riding lessons? Not Ralph! He tried pushing himself along with his feet. This was not nearly fast enough, but it was better than nothing. He moved his feet faster along the tabletop and then lifted them up while he coasted. Feeling braver, he bent low over the handlebars and worked his feet still faster toward the edge of the bedside table. When he worked up a little speed he would coast around the corner. He scrabbled his feet on the tabletop to gain momentum. In a split second he would steer to the left—

At that moment the bell on the telephone rang half a ring, so close that it seemed to pierce the middle of Ralph's bones. It rang just that half ring, as if the girl at the switchboard realized she had rung the wrong room and had jerked out the cord before the ring was finished.

That half a ring was enough. It shattered Ralph's nerves and terrified him so that he forgot all about steering. It jumbled his

thoughts until he forgot to drag his heels for brakes. He was so terrified he let go of the handgrips. The momentum of the motor-cycle carried him forward, over the edge of the table. Down, down through space tumbled Ralph with the motorcycle. He tried to straighten out, to turn the fall into a leap, but the motorcycle got in his way. He grabbed in vain at the air with both paws. There was nothing to clutch, nothing to save him, only the empty air. For a fleeting instant he thought of his poor old Uncle Victor. That was the instant the motorcycle landed with a crash in the metal waste-basket.

Ralph fell in a heap beside the motorcycle and lay still.

3

TRAPPED!

Even though Ralph woke up feeling sick and dizzy, his first thought was of the motorcycle. He hoped it was not broken. He sat there at the bottom of the wastebasket until the whirly feeling in his head stopped and he was able, slowly and carefully, to stand up. He stretched each aching muscle and felt each of his four legs to make certain it was not broken.

When Ralph was sure that he was battered but intact he examined the motorcycle. He set it upright and rolled it backward and forward to make sure the wheels still worked. One handlebar was bent and some of the paint was chipped off the rear fender, but everything else seemed all right. Ralph hoped so, but there was no way he could find out until he figured out how to start the engine. Now he ached too much even to try.

Wearily Ralph dragged himself over to the wall of his metal prison and sat down beside the apple core to rest his aching body. He leaned back against the side of the wastepaper basket, closed his eyes, and thought about his Uncle Victor. Poor nearsighted Uncle Victor. He, too, had landed in a metal wastepaper basket, jumping there quite by mistake. Unable to climb the sides, he had been trapped until the maid came and emptied him out with the trash. No one knew for sure what had happened to Uncle Victor, but it was known that trash in the hotel was emptied into an incinerator.

Ralph felt sad and remorseful thinking about his Uncle Victor getting dumped out with the trash. His mother had been right after all. His poor mother, gathering crumbs for his little brothers and sisters while he, selfish mouse that he was, sat trapped in a metal prison from which the only escape was to be thrown away like an old gum wrapper.

Ralph thought sadly of his comfortable home in the mousehole. It was a good home, untidy but comfortable. The children who stayed in Room 215 usually left a good supply of crumbs behind, and there was always water from the shirts hung to drip-dry beside the washbasin. It should have been enough. He should have been content to stay home without venturing out into the world looking for speed and excitement.

Outside in the hall Ralph heard footsteps and Matt, the bellboy, saying, "These new people in 215 and 216, somehow they got the idea there are mice in the hotel. I just opened the window and told them the management wouldn't stand for it."

Ralph heard a delighted laugh from the second-floor maid, a college girl who was working for the summer season. "Mice are adorable but just the same, I hope I never find any in my rooms. I'm afraid of them." There were two kinds of employees at the Mountain View Inn—the regulars, none of them young, and the summer help, who were college students working during the tourist season.

"If you don't like mice you better stay away from that knothole under the window in Room 215," advised Matt.

The sound of voices so close made Ralph more eager than ever to escape. "No!" he shouted, his voice echoing in the metal chamber. "I won't have it! I'm too young to be dumped out with the trash!"

In spite of his aches he jumped to his feet, ran across the wastebasket floor, and leaped against the wall, only to fall back in a sorry heap. He rose, backed off, and tried again. There he was on the floor of the wastebasket a second time. It was useless, utterly useless. He did not have the strength to tip over the wastebasket.

Ralph was not a mouse to give up easily. He considered his problem a moment before he rolled the motorcycle over to the wall of the wastebasket. Then he seized the apple core by the stem and dragged it over to the motorcycle. By putting his shoulder under the stem end, he managed to raise the core until it was standing on its blossom end, but when he put his front paws around it and tried to lift it, he found he could not. The core was too heavy to lift up onto the seat of the motorcycle. Ralph was disappointed but when he stopped to think it over, he saw that even if he could manage to get the apple core on top of the motorcycle, it still would not be high enough to allow him to climb out of the wastebasket.

Bruised and defeated, Ralph dropped the core and decided that he might as well be thrown out with the trash on a full stomach as an empty one. He took a bite of apple and felt a little better. It was the best food he had eaten for several days—juicy and full of flavor and much better than the damp zwieback crumbs the last guests had left behind. He took several more bites and settled down to a hearty meal, saving the seeds for dessert.

Two ant scouts appeared on the rim of the wastebasket.

"Go away," said Ralph crossly, because

he did not like to eat food crawling with ants and because it embarrassed him to be seen in such a predicament. The ants left as silently as they had come.

When Ralph had eaten his fill of the apple he curled up beside the core. He only hoped that someone might happen to drop a Kleenex over him. It was bad enough to be carried to one's doom in a wastebasket, but to be carried to one's doom by a shriek-ing maid was unthinkable. There was one tiny ray of hope—if someone did happen

to drop a Kleenex over him, he just might have a chance to jump and run when the maid tipped the basket up to empty it into the incinerator.

The thought that the boy was sure to miss his motorcycle and start looking for it kept Ralph tossing and turning behind the apple core until, stuffed and exhausted, he finally fell asleep.

4

KEITH

Ralph did not know how much time had passed before he was awakened by the lamp on the bedside table shining down on him. He squeezed himself into the tiniest possible ball, wrapped his tail around his body, and tried to make himself as thin as the apple core.

"My motorcycle!" shouted the boy the very first thing. "Somebody stole my motorcycle!"

Oh-oh, thought Ralph. It won't be long now.

"Nobody stole your motorcycle," answered the boy's mother from 216. "It's around someplace. You just mislaid it. You can find it in the morning. You had better get ready for bed now."

"No, I didn't mislay it," insisted the boy. "I put it right here on the table beside my sports car."

"You'll find it someplace," said his mother, not much interested. Boys were always losing things.

While Ralph cowered behind the apple core, Keith opened the drawer of the bed-side table and slammed it shut. He jerked back the bedspread, yanked the pillows off the bed, and threw them back. Then he got down on his hands and knees and looked under the bed and the table.

Ralph wrapped his tail more tightly around his body. Here it comes, he thought.

The boy's face appeared in the opening at the top of the wastebasket. Ralph's heart raced like a motor.

"Ha," said the boy to himself. "Here it is. I wonder how it got there." His hand came down into the wastebasket to seize the motorcycle and lift it out. Still leaning over the wastebasket, he examined the bent handlebar and the chipped paint. "That's funny," he remarked aloud. "It must have rolled off, but I don't see how it could."

The boy did the natural thing for a boy to do. He looked into the wastebasket again. Ralph closed both eyes tight and waited. He wished he had not eaten so much of the apple core. If he had not been so greedy, the core would have been thicker and he would have been thinner.

"Hey!" whispered the boy, obviously very much surprised. "How did you get in here?" He was careful to keep his voice lower than the sound of the breezes in the pines outside the window.

Ralph did not move. He was grateful to the boy for not touching the apple core even though it was really no protection at all.

"Psst!" whispered the boy. "Are you asleep?"

Still Ralph remained motionless except for a slight quiver of his whiskers, which he was unable to control. The boy was silent, but the mouse could feel the rhythmic drafts of his breathing. The boy must be thinking, but what was he thinking? That was what was worrying Ralph. "No," said the boy to himself. "No, it couldn't be."

Couldn't be what? wondered Ralph, who was beginning to feel cramped from crouching behind the apple core.

"Hey, wake up," whispered the boy.

That was the last thing Ralph wanted to do.

"Come on," pleaded the boy. "I won't hurt you."

Ralph considered. After all, what did he have to lose? If he stayed in the wastebasket, he was almost certain to get dumped into the incinerator. He might as well come out from behind the core. If he did he might find some opportunity to escape. Cautiously he moved his head from his paws and opened one eye. The boy was smiling down at him. Encouraged, Ralph opened the other eye and lifted his head.

"That's the stuff," encouraged the boy. "Now come on. Tell me, did you or didn't you ride my motorcycle off the bedside table?"

This took Ralph by surprise. He had not expected the boy to guess what happened. "Well, yes. I guess you might say I did," confessed Ralph, rubbing his aching muscles.

"I thought so." Neither the mouse nor

the boy was the least bit surprised that each could understand the other. Two creatures who shared a love for motorcycles naturally spoke the same language. "That must have been some accident. Did it hurt much?"

"Oh, some," answered Ralph with a display of bravado. "Anyway, I didn't exactly ride it. I really coasted off. The telephone rang and startled me. Now how about getting me out of here?"

"Just a minute," said the boy. "How did you get up here in the first place?"

"Climbed, stupid. On the telephone cord." Ralph instantly regretted his rudeness. He had better watch his tongue if he expected any help in escaping from the wastebasket.

"Oh, of course," said the boy apologetically. "I should have thought of that myself."

At that moment there came a quick knock on the door to Room 215 and the rattle of a key.

"Help!" cried Ralph. "The maid! Don't let her see me!"

Before the boy could do anything, the maid burst into the room. "Oh—excuse me." She seemed surprised to see a boy kneeling by the wastebasket. "I've come to turn down the bed."

"That's all right," said the boy quickly. "I can do it myself. Thanks, anyway."

"Thank you," said the maid, backing out of the room. Ralph knew she was not anxious to waste time turning down the bed. As soon as she finished her duties she was going out to the parking lot to meet a busboy, a college boy whose job was clearing tables in the dining room.

"Whew! That was close." The boy seemed every bit as relieved as Ralph.

"I'll say," agreed the mouse.

"Keith," called his mother from 216. "Are you getting ready for bed?"

"Sort of," answered Keith.

"You'd better come in our bathroom and take a bath," said his mother.

"Aw, gee, Mom, do I gotta?" asked Keith.

"Yes, you do," said his father.

"And don't forget to brush your teeth," said his mother.

"I won't," promised Keith. Then he whispered to Ralph, "You just lie low. I'll hurry and take a bath and get into bed and turn out the light and after Mom comes and kisses me good night, we can talk some more."

Lie low indeed! Ralph was indignant. He couldn't lie much lower if he wanted to, and he certainly did not want to sit around waiting to talk. He wanted to get out of that wastebasket. Once he was out he would see about talking, but not before.

Ralph could hear the boy splashing in 216's bathtub and then hastily brushing his

37

teeth in 215's washbasin. After this there was the sound of a suitcase being opened and clothes dropped on the floor. The boy hopped into bed and to Ralph's relief, the light was turned out. In a moment Mrs. Gridley came in to kiss her son good night.

"Night, Mom," said the boy, sounding as if he were already drowsy.

"Good night, Keith," said his mother. "It looks as if we are going to have to stay here for a few days. Your father refuses to budge."

"That's OK," muttered Keith, giving the impression he was almost asleep.

"Good boy," said his mother. "You're a good sport."

"Good night, Son," said the boy's father from the doorway between the two rooms.

Keith did not answer. Instead he breathed slowly and deeply and, as Ralph thought, a bit too noisily. There was no sense in over-doing things.

As soon as all was quiet in the next room, the boy swung his legs out of bed, fumbled around in his suitcase, and shone a flashlight into the wastebasket.

Almost blinded by the unexpected light, Ralph held his paws over his eyes. "Hey, cut that out!" He could not remember to be polite.

"Oh—sorry." The boy laid the flashlight on the bed, where its beam shone across the wastebasket rather than into it.

"That's better," said Ralph. "Now how about getting me out of here?" As an after-thought he added, "Please."

The boy ignored the mouse's request. "How would you like to ride my motor-cycle?" he asked.

Ralph's heart skipped a beat like a motor missing on one cylinder. The mouse-sized motorcycle really would run after all! And there was one thing certain. Since the motorcycle really would run, the boy could not expect him to ride around the bottom of a wastebasket. "Sure." Ralph tried to sound calm. The important thing was to get out of this prison. He braced himself, dreading the touch of the boy's hand on his fur.

To Ralph's surprise, the boy did not reach in and grab him. Instead, he slowly and gently tipped the wastebasket on its side, permitting Ralph to walk to freedom with pride and dignity.

"Thanks," said Ralph, genuinely grateful for this consideration. "I believe you're OK."

"Sure I'm OK," said the boy, setting his motorcycle down beside Ralph. "Did you think I wasn't?"

"You never can tell." Ralph put his paw on the handlebar of the motorcycle. "It's a real beauty. Even with a bent handlebar. I'm sure sorry about that."

"Forget it," said the boy reassuringly. "It

won't hurt much. The motorcycle will still run."

Ralph threw his leg over the motorcycle and settled himself comfortably in the seat.

"Perfect! Just perfect!" The boy was obviously delighted that his motorcycle was just right for a mouse.

Ralph could not have agreed more heartily. It *was* perfect—except for one thing. He did not know how to start it.

"Well, go on," said the boy. "Ride it."

Ralph was ashamed to confess his ignorance. "I don't know how to start it," he admitted. "It's the first motorcycle I have ever had a chance to ride."

"You have to make a noise," the boy explained matter-of-factly. "These cars don't go unless you make a noise."

The answer was so obvious Ralph was disgusted with himself for not knowing without asking. He grasped the handgrips and, fearful lest his noise be too squeaky, managed a *pb-pb-b-b-b*. Sure enough, the motorcycle moved. It really and truly moved across the threadbare carpet. Ralph was so excited that he promptly forgot to make the noise. The motorcycle stopped. Ralph started it again. *Pb-pb-b-b-b*. This time he remembered to keep on making the noise. He sped off into a square of moonlight on the carpet and found a good threadbare spot without any bumps.

"Look out for your tail," said the boy. "Don't let it get caught in the spokes."

"Thanks for reminding me," said Ralph, causing the motorcycle to stop. He started it again and steered with one paw while he reached back with the other, caught up his tail, and held the tip safely against the handlebar. It was a glorious sensation, speeding around on the carpet, freely and noisily and, most of all, fast. Ralph discovered that if he made the noise fast, the motorcycle speeded up. If he slowed the sound, the motorcycle slowed down. He promptly speeded up and raced around in the rectangle of moonlight, where he made another discovery. When he ran out of breath, the momentum of the motorcycle carried him on until he could take another breath.

"Gee, you're lucky," whispered the boy.

In order to answer, Ralph had to stop.

"I am?" It had never occurred to him that a mouse could be luckier than a boy.

"You sure are." The boy spoke with feeling. "My mother would never let me ride a motorcycle. She would say I might break a leg or something silly like that."

"Well, if you want to come right down to it," said Ralph, "I don't suppose my mother would be exactly crazy about the idea." He began to have an uneasy feeling that he really should be getting back to the mousehole.

"Anyway," said the boy gloomily, "it will be years and years before I'm old enough to ride a motorcycle, and then when I am old enough my mother won't let me."

Ralph really felt sorry for the boy, hampered as he was by his youth and his mother.

"Go on, ride it some more," said the boy. "I like to watch."

Pb-pb-b-b-b. Ralph started the motorcycle

again and rode around in the moonlight once more, faster and faster, until he was dizzy from circling, dizzy with excitement, dizzy with the joy of speed. Never mind the danger, never mind what his mother thought. This was living. This was what he wanted to do. On and on and on.

"Lucky," whispered the boy with envy in his voice.

Ralph did not answer. He did not want to stop.

5

ADVENTURE
IN THE NIGHT

When Ralph had mastered riding the motorcycle on the threadbare carpet, he went bumping over the roses on the less worn parts under the dresser and the bedside table. That was fun, too.

"Hey," whispered the boy. "Come on out where I can see you."

Pb-pb-b-b-b. Ralph shot out into the moonlight, where he stopped, sitting jauntily on the motorcycle with one foot resting on the floor. "Say," he said, "how about letting me take her out in the hall? You know, just for a little spin to see how fast she'll go."

"Promise you'll bring it back?" asked Keith.

"Scout's honor," answered Ralph, who had picked up many expressions from children who had stayed in 215.

"OK, I'll tell you what," said Keith. "You can use it at night and I'll use it in the daytime. I'll leave the door open an inch so you can get in. That way you can ride it up and down the hall at night."

"Can I really?" This was more than Ralph had hoped for. "Where do you want me to park it when I come in?" he asked.

"Someplace where the maid won't step on it," answered the boy.

"That's easy. Under the bed. She practically never cleans under the bed."

"Yes, I know," agreed Keith. "I looked. There are a lot of dust mice back there."

"Please—" Ralph was pained.

"Oh. Sorry," said the boy. "That's what my mother calls bunches of dusty fluff under the bed."

"*My* mother doesn't," said Ralph. "Now how about opening the door?"

The boy put his hand on the doorknob. "You won't let anything happen to my motorcycle, will you?" he asked.

"You know I wouldn't let anything happen to a beauty like this," said Ralph.

"See that you don't. And don't stay out too late." The boy opened the door and permitted Ralph to putt out into the dim light of the hall.

Ralph had a scary feeling he was on the threshold of adventure. There were no beds or chairs for him to dart under in case of danger. The floor creaked. Someone was

snoring in Room 214 across the hall. Outside in the pines an owl hooted, sending prickles up Ralph's spine.

Ralph controlled the trembling of his paws while he hesitated outside the door to consider the possibilities of the hall, which was carpeted down the center, leaving two smooth highways of bare floor on either side along the baseboards. It did not take Ralph long to decide what to do. He picked up his tail, took a deep breath, bent low over the handlebars, flattened his ears, and sped down the straightaway as fast as the motorcycle would go. He could feel his whiskers swept back by the force of his speed. It was glorious!

Ralph had never ventured so far from home before. The old wooden hotel, cooling in the night air, snapped and creaked, but Ralph was brave. He was riding a motorcycle. He passed Room 213, ran out of breath, and let momentum carry him past another noisy snorer in Room 211, on down the hall to the elevator, the mysterious elevator that carried people to that wonderful place Ralph had heard so much about—the ground floor.

When Ralph came to the stairs he stopped to look down, knowing it was impossible to ride a motorcycle downstairs and at the same time wishing he could see for himself the wonders that lay below. He sniffed the air and it seemed to him that he could smell the strange foods he had heard about—cinnamon buns with sticky frosting, turkey stuffing, and pancakes with maple syrup. A ray of moon-light from a window glinted on the glassy eye of a mounted deer's head over the stair landing and startled Ralph, sending him off down the hall, past the broom closet and the linen room to the end of the hall, where he executed a sharp turn and started back.

Exhilarated by speed, Ralph raced up and down. Once when he heard some people getting out of the elevator he had to duck behind the curtain of the window at the end of the hall. Toward midnight he passed his Aunt Sissy scurrying along the baseboard. He waved and nearly lost control of the motorcycle. Aunt Sissy stopped to stare while Ralph rode on, feeling pleased with himself and at the same time sorry for Aunt Sissy, poor frightened thing with only her feet to carry her from one crumb to the next.

Up and down the hall raced Ralph until, after an especially noisy burst of speed outside Room 211, he was startled to hear a dog bark inside the room.

Now it was Ralph's turn to be frightened. Oh-oh, he thought, I'd better be careful. If there was one thing Ralph disliked, it was people who traveled with dogs.

Dogs always sniffed around where they had no business sniffing. Once a dog had even barked into the mousehole in Room 215. It was days before Ralph's mother got over *that*.

Ralph heard someone moving around inside Room 211 and, looking back over his shoulder, he saw the door open and a tousled man in a bathrobe and slippers appeared carrying a little terrier. The man looked cross and sleepy as he started down the hall toward the elevator with his dog. He was walking straight toward Ralph.

Pb-pb-b-b-b. Realizing he was taking a chance, Ralph speeded up the motorcycle. If he turned and headed back to Room 215 he would have to pass the man. It was better to continue toward the elevator and hope he could find a place to hide. He raced on down the hall.

The wild barks of the little terrier told

Ralph that he had been seen by the dog if not by the man.

"Shut up," muttered the man to his dog. "I'm going to walk you, you don't have to wake up the whole hotel."

Ralph reached the elevator, where he drove around behind the ashtray on a stand beside the door. He stopped and waited, tense and frightened. Outside an owl hooted, was silent, and hooted again. A sudden breeze rattled windows and banged a door. Ralph's teeth began to chatter.

The dog whimpered but the man walked straight past Ralph, pushed a button, and in

a moment stepped into the elevator.

Whew! thought Ralph when the elevator door had closed on the sleepy man and his noisy dog. Maybe he had better lie low for a while. In a few minutes the elevator returned to the second floor. As the man stepped out, the little dog looked over his shoulder and spied Ralph parked behind the ashtray stand.

Because the dog was a captive and he was free, Ralph could not resist sticking out his tongue and waggling his paws in his ears, a gesture he had learned from children in Room 215 and one he knew was sure to arouse anger.

"Let me at him," barked the little terrier.

"Cut it out," grumbled the man, fumbling for the doorknob of Room 211 while Ralph, a daredevil now, rode in a giddy circle around the ashtray stand. He had a feeling of cockiness he had never known before. Who said mice were timid? Ha!

When the morning song of birds in the pines grew louder than the snores of the guests and dawn slipped through the window at the end of the hall, Ralph knew it was time to return to Room 215. There he was shocked to discover the door shut. Only then did he recall the draft in the night and the slam of a door. He got off the motorcycle and pounded on the door with his fist, but what sleeping boy could hear a mouse beating on a door?

Ralph knew from experience that he could flatten himself out and crawl under the door of Room 215, but there was no way he could get the motorcycle through the crack, not even by laying it on its side and pushing. The handlebars were too wide.

Ralph dismounted from the motorcycle, sat down, and leaned back against the baseboard, prepared to guard the motorcycle until Keith awoke and discovered the door blown shut. He was tired after a night of such great excitement and full of dreams. Now that he had seen the hall he could no longer be satisfied with Room 215. It was not enough. He longed to see the rest of the world—the dining room and the kitchen and the storeroom and the garbage cans out back. He wanted to see the game room where, he had been told, grown-up people played games with cards and balls and paddles. He wanted to go outdoors and brave the owls to hunt for seeds. Ralph, a growing mouse who needed his rest, dozed off against the baseboard beside the motor-cycle. After the experiences of this night, he would never be the same mouse again.

The next thing Ralph knew, Matt the bellboy was standing over him. "Aren't you out pretty late?" Matt asked, causing Ralph to jump to his feet even though he was not entirely awake. "You should have been in bed long ago, but I suppose you were out till all hours, speeding around on that motorcycle."

Ralph had seen Matt many times, but this was the first time the old man had spoken to him. He was astonished to discover they spoke the same language. Even so, Ralph stood in front of the motorcycle. Anyone who tried to take it away from him would have to fight Ralph first.

"Nice little machine you got there," remarked Matt. "Kind of wish I was young enough to ride one myself. Must be fun, speeding along, making all that noise."

Ralph realized that Matt was a friend. "Say," he began, "how about helping a fellow out?"

"Sure," agreed Matt. "What can I do for you?"

"Open that door a crack. Just enough

so I can ride through. I promised the boy I would park his motorcycle under the bed."

"Good place," said Matt. "The maid never cleans there if she can help it." Very quietly he turned the knob and opened the door just enough for Ralph to ride through.

Ralph bumped up over the edge of the carpet, swung out around the wastebasket and the bedside table, and was about to drive under the bed when—

"E-eek!" screamed the boy's mother, who was standing in the doorway between 215 and 216 in her bathrobe with her hair up on rollers. "A mouse!"

Ralph put on a burst of speed and shot under the bed.

"Where?" asked the boy's father, coming in from Room 216.

"Under the bed."

"I'll look, Mom," said the boy, jumping out of bed.

Keith's face appeared under the lifted edge
of the bedspread, where Ralph sat trembling
on the motorcycle. The boy held out his
hand and beckoned. Ralph understood. He

dismounted and ran up the boy's arm inside the sleeve of his pajamas until he came to the crook of his elbow. There he waited, shivering, to see what would happen next. Down at the end of the sleeve he could see the boy's fingers close around the motorcycle. Then he felt himself being lifted as the boy rose from his hands and knees.

"It's just my motorcycle," Keith said.

"Yes! That's it," agreed his mother. "The door opened and the mouse rode in—"

The boy's father began to laugh. "You are still dreaming."

"But I'm positive—" insisted the boy's mother.

"That you saw a mouse on a little red motorcycle," finished the boy's father, and laughed even harder.

"You make it sound so ridiculous," objected the mother.

"Well?" The father snorted with laughter.

"Well, perhaps I was dreaming," admitted the mother reluctantly, "but I know I saw a mouse. I'm positive and I am going to report it to the management. I knew the minute we moved into this spooky old place that it had mice."

Now I've done it, thought Ralph inside the pajama sleeve.

6

A PEANUT BUTTER SANDWICH

"I told you to be careful," scolded Keith, when his parents had gone to dress and Ralph had crawled down his arm into his hand.

"It wasn't my fault the door blew shut." Ralph jumped from the hand to the bedspread. Though Keith was a friendly boy, even a generous one, Ralph still did not like the feel of skin against his paws. It must be terrible to go through life without fur and such a nuisance, having to wear clothes that had to be washed and drip-dried. Ralph knew all about drip-drying. Many were the drops of water from shirts and slips that he had dodged going in and out of his mouse-hole.

"You didn't have to stay out so long," Keith pointed out as he began to dress.

"What's the use of having a motorcycle if you can't go tearing around staying out late?" Ralph asked reasonably.

"You don't have a motorcycle," said Keith. "I just let you use mine. And you better be careful. I like that motorcycle and I don't want anything to happen to it."

"I'll take care of it," promised Ralph, somewhat chastened. "I don't want anything to happen to it either."

"It's going to be harder to get a chance to ride it now that my mother has seen you," said Keith. "She's a terribly good house-keeper and she's sure to complain to the management."

"Speaking of breakfast, you people are too tidy," complained Ralph. "I'm not getting enough to eat around here. You don't leave any crumbs."

"I never thought of it," said Keith. "What would you like to eat?"

Ralph was astounded. This was the first time in his life anyone had asked him what he would like to eat. It had always been a question of what he could get his paws on. "You mean I have a choice?" he asked, incredulous.

"Sure," said the boy. "All I have to do is order it when we go down to breakfast and then bring you some."

Ralph had to take time to think. After a diet of zwieback and graham crackers provided by little children, bits of candy and an occasional peanut or apple core left by medium-sized children, or a crust of toast and a dab of jam left by an adult who had ordered breakfast sent up from room service, the possibilities of choosing his own meal were almost too much.

"I know what I'd like," Ralph said at last, "but I don't know what you call it. Once some people who said they were almost out of money stayed in these rooms. They had four children, all of them hungry, and they couldn't afford to go to the dining room so they got some bread and spread it with something brown out of a jar and put some more bread on top of that. They whispered all the time they were eating, because they didn't want the maid or bellboy to know they were having a meal in their room. Afterwards they all got down on their hands and knees and picked up every single crumb on the carpet so no one would guess they had eaten in their rooms. It was a great disappointment. It smelled so good. Like peanuts only better."

The boy laughed. "It was a peanut butter sandwich. Sure, I'll bring you a peanut butter sandwich. Or part of one. I'll eat part of it myself. It'll be kind of a funny breakfast, but I won't mind that."

"Where will you leave it?" asked Ralph.

Keith thought a minute. "Where do you live?" he asked.

"In the knothole under the window."

"No kidding!" Keith laughed. "That's the hole I poked my finger in last night."

"I'll say you did," said Ralph. "Scared me out of a year's growth. Nobody has ever guessed it's a mousehole because it's a knothole instead of a chewed hole."

"I tell you what," said Keith. "I'll bring up part of a peanut butter sandwich and poke it through the knothole."

"Just like room service!" Ralph could not have been more pleased with the suggestion. "Uh—what about the motorcycle?" he asked. "Where are you going to leave that?"

"In my suitcase, I guess."

"Aw, come on," pleaded Ralph. "Have a heart. Leave it someplace where I can get it while you're out during the day."

"You're supposed to be in your mousehole asleep, not riding around in the daylight where people can see you."

"Well, gee whiz, can't a fellow even look at it?" asked Ralph. "I bet you like to look at big motorcycles yourself."

"Yes, I do," admitted the boy. "Well—I'll leave it back under the bed like I said, but you promise not to ride it until after dark."

"Scout's honor." Ralph jumped off the bed and ran off to the knothole.

Ralph's home was furnished with a clutter of things people drop on the floor of a hotel room—bits of Kleenex, hair, ravelings. His mother was always planning to straighten it out, but she never got around to it. She was always too busy fussing and worrying. Now, as Ralph expected, she was dividing Ry-Krisp crumbs among his squeaky bunch of little brothers and sisters while she waited to scold him.

"Ralph, if I have told you once, I have told you a thousand times—" she began.

"Guess what!" interrupted Ralph in an attempt to change the subject. "Somebody in 215 is going to bring us a real peanut butter sandwich!"

"Ralph!" cried his frightened mother. "You haven't been associating with *people*!"

"Aw, he's just a boy," said Ralph, deciding to keep the complete story of the dangers and the glories of the past night to himself. "He wouldn't hurt us. He likes mice."

"But he's a *person*," said his mother.

"That doesn't mean he has to be bad,"
said Ralph. "Just like Pop used to say,
people shouldn't say all mice are timid just
because some mice are. Or that all mice play
when the cat's away just because some do."

"Just the same, Ralph," said his mother.
"I do wish you would be more careful

whom you associate with. I am so afraid you'll fall in with the wrong sort of friends."

"I'm growing up," said Ralph. "I'm getting too old to hang around a mouse nest all the time. I want to go out and see the world. I want to go down on the ground floor and see the kitchen and the dining room and the storeroom and the garbage cans out back."

"Oh, Ralph," cried his mother. "Not the ground floor. Not all the way down there. You aren't old enough."

"Yes, I am," said Ralph stoutly.

"There's no telling what you might run into down there—mousetraps, cats, poison. Why, out by the garbage cans you might even be seen by an owl."

"I don't care," said Ralph. "Someday I'm going downstairs."

"But think of the owls, Ralph," implored his mother. "We moved into the hotel because of the owls. It was after your Uncle

Leroy disappeared and his bones were found in an owl pellet—"

The mother mouse's plea was interrupted by the sound of Keith returning to Room 215. "Now you'll see," said Ralph to his mother and waited, anxious lest his friend let him down.

Sure enough, Keith came to the knothole. "Psst!" he whispered. "Here it is. The waitress thought I was crazy, ordering a peanut butter sandwich along with my cornflakes for breakfast, but here it is." He stuffed half a sandwich a bit at a time into the hole, where Ralph seized the pieces and pulled them all the way through. "Listen, we're going to be gone most of the day. The dining room is packing us a picnic lunch, and we're going to drive along some of the back roads and visit some old mining towns."

"Thanks a lot!" Ralph managed to say

with his mouth watering. "Have fun."

"See you tonight," said Keith. "Have a good day's sleep."

Ralph's mother could not help being impressed by the sight of that peanut butter sandwich. "Just like room service," she marveled. "Why, it's a peanut butter and *jelly* sandwich and it even has butter in it."

"I told you he would bring it." Ralph could not help boasting, even though his mouth was full.

After sharing his feast with his squeaky little brothers and sisters, all of whom had trouble with peanut butter sticking to their teeth, Ralph curled up on a heap of shredded Kleenex and took a good long nap. When he awoke refreshed, his first thought was of the motorcycle. He wondered if Keith really had remembered to leave it under the bed. He yawned and stretched and left by way of the knothole.

Room 215 was just as Ralph had last seen

it. The bed had not been made and there were no fresh towels by the washbasin. Ralph ducked under the sheets and blankets that had tumbled off one side of the bed, and there in the dim light he caught the gleam of chromium exhaust pipes. Keith had trusted him after all! He walked across the carpet and took hold of the handgrips once more. They felt just right in his paws and he longed to be off, speeding around the threadbare spots on the carpet, but a promise was a promise. Keith had kept his promise about the peanut butter sandwich; Ralph would keep his about not riding the motorcycle in the daytime. He tried to satisfy himself by walking around the motorcycle in the dim light under the bed, admiring all over again the sleek design of the machine.

Ralph was lost in admiration and day-dreams of speed and power when suddenly the door opened and the maid entered. It was too late to make a dash for the mouse-hole. The maid stripped the blankets and sheets from the beds, shedding unwelcome light on Ralph and the motorcycle. Her feet in white sneakers moved lightly as she gathered up the sheets and pillowcases and towels and dropped them with a soft plop beside the open door.

The next thing Ralph knew, he was hearing familiar and dreaded footsteps coming down the hall, steps he had learned to fear when he was a tiny mouse. It was the head housekeeper, the woman who was in charge of all the maids in the hotel. He recognized her steps and he recognized her shoes— stout, sensible black oxfords. Nothing was ever clean enough for the head housekeeper, and Ralph's whole family lived in dread lest she discover their mousehole. Now he held his breath, hoping she would go on down the hall, but no, she stepped into Room 215.

"Good morning, Margery." The house-keeper spoke crisply to the maid. "Be sure you clean 215 and 216 very thoroughly this morning. There has been a complaint from the guests. They suspect mice."

"Yes, ma'am," said the maid.

"Look behind all the drawers," continued the housekeeper, "and in the corners of the closets. Please report any evidence of mice. And be sure you vacuum under the beds. You have been getting careless lately." With that she walked briskly down the hall.

"Old grouch," muttered the maid, as she reached into the hall for something that produced a sound that struck terror into Ralph's heart.

It was the clang of vacuum cleaner attachments banging together.

7

THE VACUUM CLEANER

From his position under the bed Ralph watched the tank of the vacuum cleaner being dragged in from the hall and listened to the clash and clang of the attachments as the maid connected a long metal tube to the nozzle at the end of the hose and fastened a carpet-cleaning part to the end of the tube. He heard her humming to herself as she plugged in the deadly machine and began to work it back and forth across the carpet.

It's nice she's so happy, thought Ralph bitterly, as he watched the hungry machine devour dust and lint that lay in its path.

The maid's feet in white sneakers moved across the room until, without bothering to bend down to see where she was cleaning, she shoved the attachment under the bed. It slid closer and closer to Ralph. To be on the safe side he pushed the motorcycle farther from the reach of the machine, but he dared not take his eyes off the attachment for even an instant. He shuddered as he watched it gobble a dust mouse, but even as he shuddered he was fascinated by the power of the motor.

The maid began to sing. "I'll give to you a paper of pins, for that's the way my love begins." The attachment fell off the end of the long tube, but the maid, whose thoughts were elsewhere, did not notice. Now Ralph could feel the machine suck in its breath and knew he was in danger of being inhaled along with the dust mice.

Recklessly the maid pushed the open end of the tube back and forth any old way. There was no guessing which way it would go next. Ralph had to run with the motorcycle to avoid that terrifying hole at the end of the tube. He ran to the right, he ran to the left, and still the maid pushed the tube around, unaware that the attachment had fallen off.

Suddenly the maid threw down the tube but did not turn off the motor. The tube landed with a bump and a bounce, and before Ralph realized what was happening the awful machine had inhaled his tail and he felt himself being pulled by suction across the carpet.

"Help!" he could not keep from squeaking, but no one heard him above the roar of the machine. He just managed to catch the rear wheel of the motorcycle as he was sucked along the carpet. He hung on with all his strength. The machine, which was strong enough to suck up a mouse, was not strong enough to suck up a mouse and a motorcycle. Ralph lay there on his stomach, hanging on for dear life and feeling his whiskers and fur swept back toward the machine.

From his position on his stomach Ralph could see the girl standing in front of the

dresser. She was smiling at herself in the mirror and arranging her hair, dreaming, no doubt, of the busboy. Ralph despaired. There was no telling how long she would stand there in that silly way. With the vacuum cleaner motor making so much noise, the housekeeper was sure to think she was busy working.

Ralph felt his paws beginning to slip. He did not know how much longer he could hold out against the machine. He had to think of something and think of it fast. With every bit of strength he had left in his body, he clung to the wheels of the motor-cycle with his left paw while he moved his right paw up to the exhaust pipe. If he could just manage to pull himself along until he could get on the motorcycle . . .

Bit by bit, hand over hand, Ralph dragged himself forward along the exhaust pipe. He knew he was making progress when he could see part of his tail once more. He reached back and yanked his tail out of the tube only to have it sucked in again. Ralph was far from being out of danger.

"I'll give to you the keys to my heart," the maid sang to herself before the mirror, now pulling her hair behind her ears, now piling it on top of her head, oblivious to the desperate struggle under the bed.

Once, Ralph's paw slipped from the exhaust pipe and he thought he was a goner until he caught the rear wheel in time to save himself. Slowly he moved forward until his entire tail was free. Things were easier when he could brace his hind foot against the spokes of the rear wheel. Slowly he rose, clinging to the machine, until he was able to grasp the handgrips and throw his leg over the seat.

Ralph felt considerably safer sitting on

the motorcycle and very much pleased with himself for having outwitted the vacuum cleaner. He was quite sure by now that the maid would never bother to look under the bed. He tried to move forward, propelling the cycle with his feet, but he found the suction from the motor behind him was too strong. This made him wonder if the motor on Keith's cycle was stronger than the pull of the machine behind him. The more Ralph thought about it, the more important it seemed to him to find out.

No, I won't. Yes, I will, Ralph argued with himself. He had promised not to ride in the daytime. Yes, but Keith did not know he would have a chance to see which was stronger, the motorcycle or the vacuum cleaner. Keith would be interested, wouldn't he? Wouldn't any boy? Riding the motor-cycle would not be reckless. It would be an important experiment. Motorcycle versus

vacuum cleaner—which would be the win-
ner? Ralph had to find out.

The maid turned abruptly from the mirror. Her feet in sneakers moved across the
floor toward the electric outlet. If she dis-
connected the vacuum cleaner there would
be no experiment. If Ralph was going to pit
one motor against the other, he had to do it
now. He would never have another chance.

Pb-pb-b-b-b. Ralph picked up his tail and
started the motor. Without taking time to
let it warm up, he gunned it with all the
breath he could inhale. The motorcycle got
off to a faster start than Ralph expected, so
fast that Ralph lost control. He shot out
from under the bed just as the vacuum
cleaner died with a long drawn-out groan.

Suddenly everything went white and
Ralph found himself bumping along in a
strange ghostly place all white and made of
cloth that seemed to be closing in on him

from every direction. Ralph had ridden straight into a pillowcase thrown on the heap of laundry the maid had dropped on the floor, and the opening of the pillowcase had fallen shut behind him.

Ralph had no idea which way was out. He dismounted from the motorcycle and beat at the cloth with his fists, but everywhere he struck it was soft and yielding. He stamped his feet only to have the cloth give softly and silently beneath him.

He began to wade through the pillowcase, tugging the motorcycle along behind him while he wondered why he had thought it so important to test the motorcycle against the vacuum cleaner. The light, filtered through unknown layers of cloth, was dim, and he sank to his knees in bed linen with every step. When he came to a seam he knew he had been wading in the wrong direction.

"Drat," muttered Ralph. He turned, still dragging the motorcycle, and tried to retrace his footsteps only to find he had no idea which way he had come. There were no landmarks. The clouds of cloth were white, billowy, and yielding in all directions. "Double drat!" He stamped his foot, only to find himself sinking deeper into the linen.

From the swishing sounds he could hear outside, Ralph knew the maid must be unfolding clean sheets over the bed. He plodded on, dragging the motorcycle, without direction and with very little hope.

"He promised to buy me a bunch of blue ribbons," sang the maid, "to tie up my bonnie brown hair."

Down the hall a door opened. Ralph heard a muffled "Wuf!" and in a moment the click of a small dog's toenails on the bare floor at the edge of the hall carpet, followed by sniffing that was dangerously close.

The little terrier began to bark. "I know you're in there!" he yipped. "Stick out your tongue and waggle your fingers at me, will you? You just wait!" Paws began to scrape at the sheets and pillowcases as if the dog were trying to dig a hole.

Ralph decided it was wiser not to talk back to the dog. He huddled, scarcely breathing, against the motorcycle.

"Well, hel*lo*, you cute little thing," said the maid, revealing to Ralph that she was even sillier than he had thought. As if there was anything cute about a terrier that could scarcely see through his own hair.

The dog went on yapping, a bit self-consciously, Ralph thought, now that he knew he was being admired by the maid. A man's steps came thumping down the hall. "Stop your racket, you pesky mutt," said the owner's voice, and Ralph knew when the barks suddenly came from above him

that the dog had been snatched up.

"Let me down and I'll dig him out," yapped the dog as he was carried away. "Just let me down for one minute and I'll show you!"

Suddenly Ralph felt himself being tumbled about in the pillowcase. He did not even have to think what to do—he automatically grabbed for the motorcycle and held on with all his strength. Even though he had been tipped upside down with his feet in the air, Ralph knew he was being lifted up inside the bundle of bed linen and carried down the hall. He lay still, his front paws locked around the front wheel of the motorcycle, waiting to see what would happen next. The maid walked a short distance to what Ralph judged to be the linen room, and there she dumped her armload of bedding before she went off to clean another room.

Ralph was deep in the hamper where no light filtered through at all. These sheets and pillowcases were on their way to the laundry, and since he had no wish to be laundered, any more than he had wished to be thrown out with the trash, there was only one thing for him to do. Start chewing. Ralph ripped into the pillowcase with his sharp teeth and in no time he had made a ragged hole, which he crawled through. When he tried to pull the motorcycle after him, he discovered the hole was too small. He had to stop and chew it bigger before he could pull the machine along with him.

Ralph chewed through another layer of cloth and then another as he worked his way upward, each time enlarging the hole for the motorcycle. His jaws began to ache and still another layer of cloth lay ahead, this time a damp bath towel, which would make slow chewing.

Ralph was forced to make a decision. Did he want to save his life or did he want to be carried off to the laundry with the motorcycle? There was only one answer. He wanted to save his life. He must abandon the motorcycle.

With aching jaws Ralph chewed onward and upward, moving faster now that he was making mouse-sized holes instead of motorcycle-sized holes. The bath towel had left an unpleasant furry taste in his mouth. Gradually light began to filter through the cloth until finally, when Ralph thought he could not force his jaws to close on one more mouthful of fiber, he emerged into daylight at the top of the hamper.

"Whew!" Ralph gasped, rubbing his aching jaws and wading across the sheets to the edge of the hamper. He leaped lightly to the floor and, hugging the baseboard, scurried down the hall to Room 215, where he flattened himself and squeezed under the door. Safe but exhausted and filled with remorse at the loss of Keith's motorcycle, Ralph dragged himself off to the mousehole to catch up on the sleep he should have had that day.

8

A FAMILY REUNION

The next thing Ralph knew, his mother was shaking him by the shoulder. "Wake up," she said. "Ralph, wake up. Room service has brought us another meal."

"Room service?" Ralph rubbed his eyes, not believing what he had heard. "Room service has brought *our* dinner?"

"Yes, a real feast. A whole blueberry muffin and a chocolate-chip cookie," said

Ralph's mother. "Get up. We are having a family reunion."

It all came back to Ralph. "Oh, room service," he said, understanding at last. "You mean the boy. Keith."

"He is room service to me." Ralph's mother sounded happy and carefree.

Ralph sat up. Already his aunts and uncles and many squeaky cousins were arriving by the secret paths in the space between the walls. It was a long time since anyone had had enough food for a family reunion, and there was rejoicing in the mouse nest for everyone but Ralph. He was thinking of the motorcycle he had lost and the promise he had broken. He had a dull, heavy feeling in the pit of his stomach and he did not feel like celebrating.

"Why, there's Ralph," squeaked his Aunt Sissy, who thought she was better than the rest of the family because she lived in the bridal suite where, she led her relatives to believe, riches of rice fell to the carpet when the bride took off her hat and the groom shook out his coat. The rest of the family knew Aunt Sissy was not as grand as she pretended to be, because very few brides and grooms came to this hotel these days. "My, how you've grown."

Ralph never knew what to say when people told him how he had grown.

"Well, well! If it isn't Ralph!" said Uncle Lester, who had a nest inside the wall of the housekeeper's office, where the maids dropped doughnut crumbs every morning at ten o'clock when they had their coffee. "What's this I hear about you riding up and down the halls on a motorcycle?" Uncle Lester had a way of saying the wrong thing at the wrong time.

"My land, a motorcycle," said old Aunt Dorothy. "Isn't that pretty dangerous?"

"Wouldn't mind riding one myself if I were a few years younger," said Uncle Lester.

All the little cousins came crowding around Ralph. "Show us your motorcycle," they squeaked. "We want to ride it. Come on, give us a ride on your motorcycle, Ralph. Huh, Ralph? Come on, Ralph. Please!"

Ralph knew he was expected to be polite to all his relatives, even the squeaky little cousins. "Well . . ." Embarrassed and ashamed, he looked down at the floor. "I sort of . . . lost the motorcycle. In a pile of sheets and pillowcases."

"Lost the motorcycle! Oh, Ralph," cried his mother, genuinely alarmed.

Ralph knew what she was thinking. Did this mean the end of room service? Did she have to go back to pilfering crumbs for his brothers and sisters?

"That's a young mouse for you," said tactless Uncle Lester. "Can't take care of anything."

"If anybody asks me, I think it's a good thing he lost it," said Aunt Dorothy. "Riding a motorcycle is just plain foolhardy."

All the little cousins looked disappointed and sulky. "I don't think he ever had a motorcycle," said one.

"I bet he just made it up," said another, and the rest agreed.

Ralph felt terrible. The family reunion swirled on around him. The muffin and cookie were divided. Cousins fought over the blueberries. Uncles, usually overweight uncles, asked for second helpings. Everyone talked at once. The little cousins finished their dinner and went racing around the mouse nest. The aunts and uncles raised their voices to be heard above the racket their children made.

Suddenly there came from the knothole a noise that drowned out the squeaks and squeals of young mice at play.

"Sh-h-h!"

Not a mouse moved. They looked at one another, too terrified to speak.

"Pst! Hey, Ralph, come on out," whispered Keith at the entrance to the mouse nest.

Ralph's mother gave him a little shove, but no one spoke. With heavy feet Ralph walked to the knothole, but he did not go out into Room 215. "What do you want?" he asked.

"You and your family better be quiet in there or my mother will hear you. You know how she is about mice," Keith said. "I don't know why people say things are as quiet as mice. You sound like a pretty noisy bunch to me."

Behind Ralph his relatives began to tiptoe

quietly away to their own homes, leaving his mother to do all the cleaning up. "Did you have a nice picnic?" Ralph asked, dreading what he must tell the boy.

"Yes. We saw an old mining town with a real jail with bars on the windows."

Keith reached into his pocket and pulled out something curved and hard and white with a rubber band fastened to it with a piece of Scotch tape. "I brought you a present," he said. "Come on out."

Puzzled and curious, Ralph squeezed through the knothole. "What is it?" he asked. Whatever the object was, he had never seen anything like it.

"Half a Ping-Pong ball I found down in the game room," said Keith. "See, I padded the inside with thistledown and anchored the rubber band to the top with Scotch tape."

"What for?" Ralph still did not understand.

"A crash helmet for you." Keith set the half Ping-Pong ball on Ralph's head and slipped the rubber band carefully around his whiskers until it rested under his chin. "There. That's just right. You need it big so there will be plenty of room for your ears. When you ride a motorcycle you need a crash helmet."

Ralph peered at Keith from under his new crash helmet, which rested lightly on his head. He knew he looked every inch a motorcycle racer, but never in his whole life had he felt so ashamed. He longed to crawl off into his hole and never face Keith again, but his conscience, which until now he did not know he had, would not let him. There was nothing to do but stand there in his fine new crash helmet and confess. "You might as well know," he told Keith. "I lost the motorcycle."

"Lost the motorcycle!" Keith, who had

been kneeling, sat back on his heels. "But how?"

"I rode it by mistake into a pillowcase in a heap of linen on the floor, and it got dumped into the laundry hamper," confessed Ralph.

"You *rode* it into the pillowcase!" repeated Keith. "But you weren't supposed to ride it in the daytime. You *promised*."

"I know," agreed Ralph miserably. "I didn't exactly mean to ride it."

"Well, you see, the maid was vacuuming under the bed and I—" began Ralph, and stopped. "Oh, what's the use. I rode it and I lost it and it's probably gone to the laundry by now and I'm sorry."

The boy and the mouse were silent. Both were thinking about the little motorcycle with its clean lines and pair of shining chromium exhaust pipes.

"That motorcycle was my very most favorite of all my cars," said Keith. "I saved my allowance and bought it myself."

Ralph hung his head in his crash helmet. There was nothing more he could say. It was a terrible thing he had done.

"I guess I should have known you weren't old enough to be trusted with a motorcycle," said Keith.

The boy could not have said anything that would hurt Ralph more.

9

RALPH TAKES COMMAND

It was a sad night for Ralph, a sad and lonely night. If he went back to the mousehole, his mother was sure to worry him with embarrassing questions about the motorcycle. She would also expect him to help clean up after the family reunion. If he took off his crash helmet, he could squeeze under the door and explore the hall on foot, but he could not bear to part with the helmet and, anyway, he had no desire to travel by foot where he had once ridden with such noise and speed.

Ralph scurried through shadows on the floor to the curtain, which he climbed to the windowsill. There he sat, huddled and alone, staring out into the night listening to the kissing sounds of the bats as they jerked and zigzagged from the eaves of the hotel, through the pines, and back again. Around the window the leaves of a Virginia creeper vine shifted in the breeze, and down in the lobby a clock struck midnight. An owl slid silently through the night across the clearing of the parking lot from one pine to another. Ralph could remember a time when he had envied bats and owls their ability to fly, but that was before he had experienced the speed and power of a motorcycle.

Early in the morning the smell of bacon drifting up from the kitchen brought back all Ralph's dreams of the ground floor. It was not long until he was embarrassed to discover that Keith was awake and was lying quietly in bed watching him.

"Hi," said Keith.

"Oh, hello." Ralph wished he had returned to the mousehole before dawn. "Well, I guess it's about time for me to go home to bed."

Keith sat up. "Don't go yet. Wait until my folks get up."

Ralph leaped to the floor. "I didn't think you would want to talk to me after I lost your motorcycle."

"I may never have another chance to talk to a mouse."

Ralph was flattered. It had never occurred to him that a boy would consider talking to a mouse anything special.

"What would you like for breakfast?" asked Keith.

"You mean we still get room service? After what I did?"

"Sure." Keith pulled his knees up under his chin and wrapped his arms around his legs.

"You mean you aren't mad at me anymore?" asked Ralph.

"I guess you might say I'm mad but not *real* mad," Keith decided. "I've been lying here thinking. It wouldn't be right for me to be *real* mad, because I get into messes myself. My mom and dad tell me I don't stop to use my head."

Ralph nodded. "I guess that's my trouble, too. I don't stop to use my head."

"They say I'm in too much of a hurry," said Keith. "They say I don't want to take time to learn to do things properly."

Ralph nodded again. He understood. If he had waited until he had learned to ride the motorcycle he would never have ridden off the bedside table into the wastebasket.

"I'll never forget the first time I rode a bicycle with hand brakes," reminisced Keith. "I took right off down a hill. I had always ridden bicycles with foot brakes, and when I got going too fast I tried to put on foot brakes only there weren't any."

"What happened?" Ralph was fascinated.

"By the time I remembered to use the hand brakes I hit a tree and took an awful spill."

Somehow, this story made Ralph feel better. He was not the only one who got into trouble.

"The hard part is," continued Keith, "I *am* in a hurry. I don't want to do kid things. I want to do big things. Real things. I want to grow up."

"You look pretty grown up to me," said Ralph.

"Maybe to a mouse," conceded Keith, "but I want to look grown up to grown-ups."

"So do I," said Ralph with feeling. "I want to grow up and go down to the ground floor."

"Everybody tells me to be patient," said Keith, "but I don't want to be patient."

"Me neither," agreed Ralph. Someone stirred next door in Room 216. "Well, I guess I better be running along," said Ralph. "Say, about that breakfast—"

"Sure. What do you want?"

"How about some bacon?" suggested Ralph, remembering the fragrance that had floated up to the windowsill.

"And some toast?"

"With jelly," agreed Ralph, and ran off to the mousehole, eager to tell his family things were not so bad after all. They were still entitled to room service.

But when Ralph reached the mousehole he found pandemonium. His brothers and sisters and cousins were huddled together

squeaking with fright. His mother picked
up a bunch of shredded Kleenex and put it
down again, only to pick up another bunch
as if she did not know what to do with it.
Uncle Lester and Aunt Dorothy were there,
too, stuffing crumbs into their mouths as if
they expected never to eat again.

"Dear me," Ralph's mother was saying,

"whatever shall we—oh Ralph, there you
are at last. Where on earth have you been?
Never mind. We haven't time—"

"Time for what?" asked Ralph. "What's
going on around here anyway?"

"The housekeeper . . . your Uncle
Lester . . . the sheets. Oh, do be quiet,
everybody." Ralph's mother was so agitated

she could not tell her son what was wrong.

Uncle Lester swallowed a mouthful of crumbs. "It's like this, Ralph. The housekeeper discovered a hamperful of sheets and towels and pillowcases with holes chewed in them."

Oh-oh, thought Ralph. Whatever had happened was all his fault. He might have known.

"I heard her telephoning the manager about it from her office," continued Uncle Lester. "The manager came up and called in all the maids and the bellboys and everyone had to look at the holes chewed in the sheets. It was quite a powwow."

The motorcycle, thought Ralph. What happened to the motorcycle? There might be a chance it did not go to the laundry after all. "You didn't happen to see a motorcycle in the housekeeper's office, did you?" he ventured.

"I was listening, not looking out," said Uncle Lester. "*I* am not foolhardy like some people around here."

"Ralph, you know what this means." His mother managed to pull herself together to say that much.

"It means *war on mice*," said Aunt Dorothy ominously.

"It means traps, poisons," said Uncle Lester. "Who knows? This time the management might even spend money on an exterminator. We shall have to flee. There is nothing else to do."

"And if we flee the owls will get us," said Ralph's mother, causing the brothers and sisters and cousins to set up an awful squeal. "Sh-h!" The mother mouse fluttered her paws in alarm.

"Flee?" Ralph was bewildered. "Flee and leave room service?"

"Room service!" exclaimed his mother.

"How can we expect room service after you lost that poor boy's motorcycle?"

"It's all right," Ralph assured his mother, and could not resist adding rather grandly, "I've already ordered. Room service is bringing us bacon and toast with jelly."

This news silenced everyone. A breakfast of bacon and toast with jelly delivered to the mouse nest without first being dropped on the carpet was not to be abandoned lightly.

"We want some jelly! We want some jelly!" all the little cousins began to squeak.

"Be quiet!" ordered Uncle Lester. "Do you want them to find us?"

Ralph knew that no matter what the others chose to do, he was not going to flee from the hotel, not until he found out what had happened to the motorcycle. He was very sure of this and all at once he felt calm and clearheaded as he had never felt before. He knew exactly what his family should do.

"Be quiet, everybody," Ralph ordered, standing up straight so all his relatives could see him. "I will tell you what we are going to do."

"See here, Ralph," interrupted Uncle Lester. "You are pretty young to be giving orders to your elders."

"Now Lester," said Aunt Dorothy. "Let's listen to Ralph. After all, he has our food brought up by room service. No one else in the history of the family has managed that."

This silenced Uncle Lester and Ralph was allowed to continue. "What we should do is keep quiet for a few days." Here he looked down at his little cousins, who for once in their lives were not squeaking. "I will arrange for room service to bring our meals so we won't have to go scrabbling around in the woodwork or scrounging around in the rooms. That way we won't be tempted to taste any poison food or go near any traps, and if the management doesn't see or hear any of us for a few days, they will forget about us. They always do."

"Now just a minute," said Uncle Lester. "This boy won't be here long. You know how it is with people. Here today and gone tomorrow."

Ralph had the answer. "This is only Sunday. He will be here until Tuesday because Monday is the Fourth of July and his father says he won't drive in holiday weekend traffic. He always brings us plenty and if we don't stuff ourselves we can save enough to last until the management forgets us."

Uncle Lester nodded thoughtfully. "That seems like a sound idea."

"Yes, but Ralph, there is one thing that worries me," said his mother. "How are we going to tip room service? When people have a waiter bring food to the room they always give him a coin or two for his service. We haven't any money."

Ralph had not thought of this.

"If we are going to continue to accept room service we must do the right thing," insisted his mother.

"Don't worry. I'll think of something," promised Ralph in the grand way he had acquired since he had ordered a meal sent up to the mouse nest.

10

AN ANXIOUS NIGHT

At first Ralph's scheme worked. Keith delivered the promised bacon, toast, and jelly; the mice ate sparingly and laid aside the leftovers against the day Keith must leave the hotel. Ralph's mother continued to worry about tipping room service. "I want to do the right thing," she insisted. "There must be some way we could manage a tip." The mice dared not leave the nest to search for small coins that might have rolled under beds and dressers.

It was late in the afternoon when Ralph heard Keith and his parents returning to their rooms. Very quietly, so that his toenails did not make scrabbling sounds in the woodwork, he slipped to the knothole and peeped out in time to see Keith flop down on the bed.

"Do I have to go down to the dining room for dinner?" Keith asked his mother and father. "I'm not hungry."

Oh-oh, thought Ralph. There goes dinner.

"I told you not to eat that whole bag of peanuts so close to dinnertime," said his father.

"I didn't eat all of it," said Keith.

That's good, thought Ralph. At least there would be peanuts for dinner.

"You'll feel better after you get washed

up for dinner," said Mrs. Gridley. "Hurry along now."

When his parents had gone into Room 216, Ralph noticed that Keith seemed to drag himself off the bed. He walked to the washbasin, turned on the cold water, moistened his fingers, and wiped them over his face. Then he turned off the water and gave the middle of his face a swipe with a towel, which he returned to the towel rack in such a way that it immediately fell to the floor. Keith did not pick it up, but there was nothing unusual about this. Boys rarely picked up towels. What was unusual was that Keith returned to the bed, where he sat down and stared at the wall. He did not play with his cars, nor did he eat the rest of his peanuts. He just sat there.

Ralph stuck his head out of the knot-hole. "Anything wrong?" he asked.

"Oh, hi," answered Keith listlessly. "I feel sort of awful."

"Say, that's too bad." Ralph ventured a little farther out of the knothole. "I know what you mean. Thinking about the motor- cycle makes me feel awful, too."

"It's not that kind of awful," said Keith.

"I feel awful in a different way. Sort of in my insides."

"Think you'll make it to dinner?" asked Ralph.

"Oh, I guess so." There was no enthusiasm in Keith's voice. "Anything I can bring you?"

"Whatever is handy," said Ralph, who hesitated to place an order when he could see Keith did not feel like going to dinner at all. "We are . . . sort of depending on you. The housekeeper found all those sheets I had to chew through to get out of the hamper, and I understand she got pretty excited about mice. We are lying low until the whole thing blows over."

A smile flickered across Keith's face. "Don't worry. I won't let you down. I saved you some peanuts. I thought they might be handy for storing."

"Gee, thanks," said Ralph.

Keith got slowly off the bed and poked the peanuts, one by one, through the knothole. When he had finished Ralph popped out again and said, "Thanks a lot."

Keith smiled feebly and flopped down on the bed once more. Ralph went to work moving the peanuts away from the knothole to make room for whatever dinner Keith brought. He felt it would be fun to be surprised by the menu this time.

It was something of a shock to find that dinner, which was stuffed through the knothole much earlier than Ralph expected, consisted of a couple of broken soda crackers.

Ralph poked his head out to see if more was coming, but Keith was getting into his pajamas.

"Aren't you going to bed pretty early?" asked Ralph, realizing he had not heard Keith's parents come in.

"I felt so awful I couldn't eat so they told

me I had better come up and go to bed." Keith tossed his shirt on the foot of the bed and pulled on his pajama top. When his head emerged, he said, "I'm sorry about your dinner. It was the best I could do. All I had was a little soup."

"That's all right." Ralph was beginning to be concerned. If the boy could not eat, neither could the mice. Keith fell into bed and Ralph ran off to report the news to his relatives.

"What a shame," said Ralph's mother. "The poor boy!"

"Oh dear, whatever shall we do?" cried Aunt Dorothy. "Our very lives depend on him." The little cousins huddled together, big-eyed and frightened.

"Yes, what about us?" asked Uncle Lester. "How are we going to manage if he doesn't bring us our meals? It isn't safe for us to go out pilfering when the housekeeper has declared war on mice."

"I knew it was a mistake to depend on people," said Aunt Sissy.

"We'll manage somehow. We always have." Ralph's mother was trying to be brave, but Ralph could see how worried she was. "After all, he did bring us a supply of peanuts. We should be grateful for that."

"He didn't bring many peanuts." Uncle Lester did not sound the least bit grateful. "The greedy fellow is probably ill from stuffing himself with nuts he should have saved for us. Serves him right."

"Now Lester," fussed Ralph's mother. "The boy had a right to eat his own peanuts, but I do wish he hadn't been quite so hungry."

Ralph returned to the knothole. Keith was lying in bed with his sports car in one hand. "How do you feel now?" asked Ralph.

"Awful," answered Keith.

Before Ralph could reply, footsteps in the hall warned him that Keith's parents were coming. He drew back inside the knothole where he could observe without being seen. Mrs. Gridley paused by her son's bed and laid her hand on his forehead. "He does feel a little warm," she remarked.

"He'll probably be all right in the morning," said Mr. Gridley. "He just hiked too far in the sun this afternoon."

"I hope so." The boy's mother sounded less certain.

Mr. Gridley filled a glass at the washbasin and brought it to Keith. "Here, Son, drink this." When Keith had drunk the water he fell back on the pillow and closed his eyes. His parents went quietly into Room 216.

When it was good and dark Ralph ventured through the knothole. He could hear Keith breathing deeply and he knew that he was asleep. Since he had no one to talk to, he found his little crash helmet where he had hidden it behind the curtain and, after he had adjusted the rubber band under his chin, he climbed up to the windowsill to look out into the world beyond the hotel and to dream about the lost motorcycle.

From his perch on the windowsill Ralph saw that the parking lot held more cars than

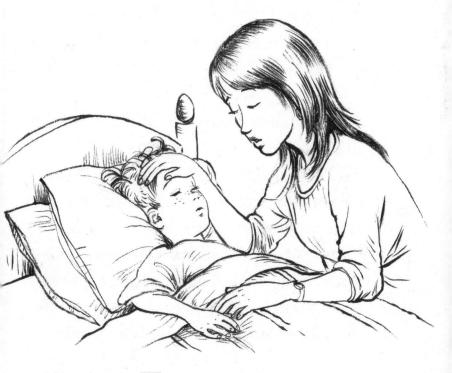

usual. This meant that the motels back on the highway were full and travelers had followed the sign pointing to the Mountain View Inn. He could hear the holiday weekend activity in the halls, too—people walking up and down, luggage being set with a thump on the floor, keys rattling in locks. Gradually, as the night wore on, the hotel grew silent, more silent than usual for now even the second-floor mice were quiet. There was no scurrying, scrabbling, or squeaking inside the walls.

In the silence Keith tossed in his sleep and mumbled something that sounded like "motorcycle." In a moment his mother slipped through the doorway, pulling her robe on over her nightgown. Ralph hid behind the curtain, peeping out just enough to see what was going to happen. She laid her hand on her son's forehead and murmured, "Oh, dear."

Almost at once she was joined by Keith's

father, who was tying the belt to his bath-robe. "What's the trouble?" he asked.

"Keith has a fever," answered the mother. "He's burning up."

Ralph was shocked. The boy really was sick. It was not too many peanuts or too much hiking. The boy was really and truly sick.

The father turned on the lamp on the bedside table and he too laid his hand on the boy's forehead. Keith opened his eyes. "I'm so hot," he mumbled. "I want a drink."

His mother pulled back a blanket while the father brought a glass of water and held up his son's head so he could drink part of it.

Ralph watched anxiously, but this time he was not selfishly concerned about room service. He was concerned about Keith, the boy who had saved him from a terrible fate in the wastebasket and who had trusted him with his motorcycle, the boy who had

forgiven him when he had lost that motorcycle and who had brought food, not only
for Ralph, but for his whole family.

"We had better give him an aspirin to
bring down his temperature," said Mrs.
Gridley.

Mr. Gridley started toward Room 216,
stopped, and snapped his fingers as if he had
just remembered something. "I took the last
one back in Rock Springs, Wyoming," he
said. "I had a headache from driving toward
the sun all afternoon. I meant to buy some
more when we stopped, but I didn't think
of it again until now."

"I should have thought of it myself," said
Mrs. Gridley. "I knew we were almost out."

"Never mind. I'll get some." Mr. Gridley picked up the telephone, listened, shook
it, listened again, and said, "That's peculiar.
The line seems to be dead."

"They must disconnect the switchboard

at night," said the mother, "but surely there is someone on duty at the desk downstairs. Every hotel has a night clerk."

"I'll go find out," said the father, and slipped out the door into the hall.

"I'm so hot," mumbled Keith. "I'm so hot."

His mother wrung out a washcloth in cold water and laid it on her son's forehead. "You'll feel better as soon as we get you an aspirin," she whispered.

The minutes dragged by. What's keeping him? thought Ralph. Why doesn't he hurry? The old hotel snapped and creaked. Keith rolled and tossed, trying to find a cool spot on the pillow, and his mother wrung out the washcloth in more cold water.

"When's Dad coming?" asked Keith, his eyes bright and his cheeks flushed.

"In a minute," soothed his mother. "He'll be here in a minute."

I wish he would hurry, thought Ralph.

Still the minutes dragged. Finally foot-steps were heard in the hall and Mr. Gridley returned to Room 215.

"He's here with the aspirin," whispered Mrs. Gridley to Keith.

At last, thought Ralph. I thought he would never come.

Mr. Gridley shook his head. "There isn't an aspirin to be found anyplace." He sounded thoroughly exasperated. "First of all, the night clerk was sound asleep on a couch in the lobby. I had a dickens of a time waking him up and when I finally did manage to, he couldn't find any aspirin anywhere."

"Oh, no!" exclaimed the mother.

Oh, no! echoed Ralph's thoughts.

"What about that little gift shop off the lobby?" asked Mrs. Gridley. "It must sell aspirin."

"Locked up tight and the clerk went

home with the key," answered Mr. Gridley.

"Oh, dear!"

"The night clerk was really very nice about it," said the father. "He even came up and looked in the housekeeper's office."

"How far is the nearest drugstore?"

"Twenty-five miles back on the main highway," answered the father. "And it closed at ten o'clock and doesn't open until nine in the morning."

The mother held her watch under the lamp. "And it is almost one o'clock. It is hours until morning." She crossed the room to wring out the washcloth again. "What will we do?"

"What can we do?" asked the father helplessly. "I even telephoned the doctor, but there has been a bad accident back on the highway and he can't come. The night clerk said he would telephone the milkman before he starts his route at six and ask him if he can bring some aspirin, but he won't get here until seven or later. All we can do is wait."

Keith tossed under the cold washcloth. "Mom, I think I'd like to go to sleep now," he muttered thickly.

"I guess that is all you can do," said his mother, and bent over to kiss his hot forehead before she turned out the light.

Ralph did not even wait for the boy's parents to leave the room. As soon as the light was out he leaped silently to the carpet, and by the time they had gone through the doorway into Room 216 he had hidden his little crash helmet behind the curtain and was halfway through the knothole. Somewhere, someplace in that hotel there must be an aspirin tablet and Ralph was going to find it. He only wished he had the motorcycle so he could travel faster.

11

THE SEARCH

"I have to go out into the hotel," Ralph informed his relatives. "I've got to help the boy."

"Oh, no, not out into the hotel," cried Ralph's mother. "Not while the house-keeper is looking for mice. If you're seen we'll all be in danger."

"I'll be back before dawn," said Ralph staunchly. "I must go. Don't try to stop me."

"See here, my boy, aren't you being a bit dramatic?" asked Uncle Lester. "Whatever do you have to go out into the hotel for?"

"To pilfer a pill," said Ralph. "An aspirin tablet." His answer was dramatic enough even for Uncle Lester. His entire family stared at him in disbelief. Not an aspirin! Not after his own father had been poisoned by one of the dread tablets.

"An aspirin!" Ralph's mother gasped. "No, Ralph, not that! Anything but that!"

"It is the only way." Ralph stood tall and brave. "The boy has a fever and he needs an aspirin. I'm going to find him one."

"Oh, Ralph!" His mother hid her face in her paws.

"But Ralph," quavered Aunt Sissy. "Remember your father. You can't carry an aspirin in your cheek pouches. It would poison you. How could you get one here?"

"I'll find a way." Ralph was outwardly steadfast in his determination, but inside he wondered how he would manage to get an aspirin into Room 215 if he did find one. Roll it, perhaps.

"Ralph, stay here," pleaded his mother. "You're too young. Let your Uncle Lester go."

"Well, now, let's talk this over," said Uncle Lester.

"I'm not too young and I haven't a moment to lose." Ralph, who was really frightened by what he was about to do, also enjoyed the drama of the moment. "Good-bye. I shall return before dawn."

"Ralph, promise me you'll be careful," pleaded his mother. "Promise me you won't climb into suitcases like your Aunt Adrienne." Ralph's Aunt Adrienne, who liked nice things, had climbed into a suit-case to examine a nylon stocking, someone had closed the suitcase, and Aunt Adrienne had never been seen again. It was hoped she had been carried away to a life of luxury. "Promise me, Ralph," cried his mother, but her son was already on his way out the knothole.

Ralph scurried across the carpet of Room 215, flattened himself, and squeezed under the door. Once out in the hall, his courage ebbed. The aspirin tablet seemed a very small thing to find in such a vast place. It would be much easier to find the motorcycle. No, thought Ralph, I must not even think about the motorcycle.

Ralph began to feel pretty small himself, much smaller than he had felt during his show of bravery back in the mouse nest. Down in the lobby a clock struck one. There was not a moment to lose. He ran to the next room, squeezed under the door, and searched under the beds and the dresser while the two guests slept soundly. All he found was a bobby pin.

He skipped Room 211 because his enemy, the little terrier, was still there, and ran on to Room 209. A hurried search, frightening because of the loud and uneven snores that came from one of the beds, revealed nothing but a few pretzel crumbs, which Ralph did not have time to eat.

On and on ran Ralph, down the hall, under doors, around under beds and dressers. There was not a single aspirin tablet to be found. In one of the rooms he did see a penny that had rolled under a luggage rack and remembered his mother's wish to leave a tip for room service, but tonight he had no time for pennies. He must press on and find an aspirin.

A small doubt began to creep into Ralph's thoughts as he ran down the hall to the last room on the second floor. Maybe there was no aspirin. Maybe he was risking his life and the lives of his family for nothing. But Ralph pushed the thought aside. He would not let himself become discouraged. If there was no aspirin on the second floor, there had to be one someplace on the ground floor. Tonight he was willing to brave the stairs to find it. He flattened himself and squeezed under the last door on the second floor. There was nothing under either of the beds but the things Keith called dust mice. There was no sound but the rattle of the windows in the wind.

Ralph started across the carpet toward the dresser when suddenly a light from the bedside table blinded him. He stopped, rooted to the carpet by fear, even though it was not likely that anyone was going to cut off *his* tail with a carving knife.

He heard someone slip out of bed and utter a sound halfway between a squeal and a scream. Before Ralph knew what was happening, an ordinary drinking glass had been clapped down over him, and there he stood in a glass trap.

By then his eyes were adjusted to the light and he found himself facing a pair of bare feet. Looking up, he saw that the feet belonged to a young woman in a pink nightgown.

"Mary Lou, wake up," she whispered to the young woman in the other bed. "Look what I've caught."

"Huh?" said Mary Lou, blinking and raising up on one elbow. Her hair was done up on pink rollers. "Betty, are you out of your mind? It must be past one o'clock in the morning."

The night was slipping by much too quickly for the trapped mouse. He was terrified and he was desperate. No one in his family had ever been trapped under a drinking glass before. Worst of all, he was failing Keith and endangering his family.

"Wake up, Mary Lou, and look," insisted Betty. "I was getting up to stop the rattle in the window and caught a mouse!"

This news roused Mary Lou from bed, and the two young women knelt on the carpet to look at Ralph, who promptly turned his back. He did not care to be stared at in his misery, but it was no use. The women moved around to the other side of the glass.

"Isn't he darling?" said Betty.

"Just look at his cunning little paws." Mary Lou leaned closer for a better look.

"And his little ears. Aren't they sweet?" Betty was delighted.

It was disgusting. It was bad enough to be trapped and stared at, but to have this pair carrying on in such a gushy fashion was almost more than Ralph could stomach. Cunning little paws indeed! They were strong paws, paws for grasping the hand-grips of a motorcycle.

"Oh, Betty, do you suppose we could take him back to Wichita with us?" asked Mary Lou. "My third grade would love him."

"So would my kindergarten," agreed Betty. "We could keep him in a cage on the ledge and all the children could bring him food from home. It would be such a good experience for them to have a pet in the classroom."

Well, thought Ralph grimly, I always wanted to travel. A cage in a kindergarten in Wichita, however, was not exactly the destination he had in mind. The minutes were slipping by dangerously fast. He had to do something. "Look," he shouted through the glass in desperation. "Let me go. Please let me go. There's something terribly important I've got to do."

"He squeaked!" marveled Betty.

"He's adorable!" squealed Mary Lou.

It was no use. Young women could not speak his language. Ralph was in despair. He thought of Keith tossing feverishly in his bed and of his family huddled in the mouse nest waiting for his safe return.

"But I don't see how we could take him back to Wichita," said Betty sensibly. "We're driving to San Francisco and then to Disneyland before we start back. How could we carry him thousands of miles?"

The two teachers looked thoughtfully at Ralph, who knew his fate depended on their decision. Was he to be carried to Disneyland and eventually to a ledge in a kindergarten room in Wichita? Or would they let him go? A third possibility crossed Ralph's mind. Perhaps they would leave him under the glass for the housekeeper to see. He hoped not. He did not think he could last that long.

Already the inside of the glass was beginning to feel warm and airless.

"I suppose we really shouldn't turn him loose in the hotel," said Mary Lou. "Mice are pests even if they are cute."

The teacher not only destroyed Ralph's hopes, she hurt his feelings as well, calling him a pest when he was on an errand of mercy. From the mouse's point of view, the teachers were the pests.

"I know!" exclaimed Betty suddenly, causing Ralph to look over his shoulder for a clue to what it was she knew. "I know how we can get rid of him without hurting him."

The young teacher reached over to the bedside table, where she picked up a picture postcard. She slid it carefully under the glass and under Ralph's feet so that he was now standing on a postcard. He noticed the picture was of a giant redwood tree, the same postcard all travelers bought when they came to California.

"Now what are you going to do?" asked Mary Lou.

"Watch." Betty carefully lifted the postcard, Ralph, and the glass, and walked across the room.

Even though he knew it was useless, Ralph scrabbled around in his tiny prison. He was afraid she was taking him toward the washbasin. He had heard of mice being drowned by people who did not like traps.

The teacher walked not to the washbasin, but to the open window. She held Ralph across the sill, removed the postcard from the glass, and gave it a little jerk that shook Ralph off into the vines that grew up the side of the building.

"There," she said, and closed the window, leaving Ralph clinging to a vine high above the ground.

12

AN ERRAND OF MERCY

Owls! thought Ralph, as he clung to the Virginia creeper and filled his lungs with the cool night air that was such a relief after the stuffy drinking glass. I've always wanted to climb down this vine and explore the ground floor, he reminded himself grimly, and now I have to. Ralph had never before been outdoors beneath the moon and the stars. He felt small and

frightened and alone.

Slowly, paw over paw, he worked his way along the shoots and tendrils. An owl, uncomfortably close in a pine tree, hooted, and Ralph huddled shivering in

 the shadow of a leaf, aware that he was losing precious seconds.

A night wind rattled the windows and the owl glided off across the parking lot. Ralph inched his way down the vine. It was a long winding route full of detours to the ground-floor window, which, to Ralph's relief, was open.

Upon reaching the sill, Ralph leaped to the floor of the room, in which three young men of college age were sleeping, two in beds and one in a sleeping bag on the floor.

An aspirin, I must find an aspirin, thought Ralph, darting under the bed. He bumped into a dust mouse, which startled him, but he did not find an aspirin. He was in such a hurry he ran right over the man in the sleeping bag instead of taking time to go around. There under the dresser, gleaming in a shaft of moonlight, he saw a round white pill. He went closer.

Yes, it really was an aspirin tablet. At last! Ralph was positive it was an aspirin and not some other pill because it had letters stamped on it. Ralph could not read the letters, but he knew they stood for an aspirin. He had been warned about them often enough. Now all Ralph had to do was figure out how to get the pill upstairs to Room 215.

Telling himself that in spite of all that had happened that night, it could not be much past one o'clock in the morning, Ralph half pushed and half rolled the aspirin tablet around the man in the sleeping bag to the door. He shoved it under the door and with great difficulty squeezed under himself. The first-floor carpet was thicker and of better quality than that of the second floor.

Ralph worked his way with the aspirin down the hall to the lobby where the night clerk was asleep on a couch. The glassy eyes of deer heads mounted on the knotty pine walls seemed to stare at Ralph. So did the giant eye of the television set. Slowly he moved his precious load across the lobby to the stairs and there he stopped. How could he manage to get that aspirin up those stairs? He picked it up and tried lifting it, even though he knew he could not reach the first step with it.

The night clerk tossed on the couch and made a gobbling, snorting noise. Ralph dropped the aspirin in a panic and looked wildly about for a hiding place. With one terrified leap he dived under the grandfather clock between the elevator and the stairs. It was immediately plain from the dust that no one ever cleaned under the clock.

"A-haa. A-haa." Ralph struggled to

control a sneeze. Above him the works of the clock began to make grinding noises.

"A-choo!" The sneeze could not be held back.

Bong! The clock struck one thirty, forcing Ralph to clap his hands over his ears. How his famous ancestor, the one that ran up the clock, hickory-dickory-dock, stood the racket, he did not know.

Peeking out, Ralph discovered the night clerk had slept soundly through the din, so he ventured out from under the clock to continue his struggle with the aspirin tablet.

Since carrying the pill up the stairs was impossible, Ralph had to find another way. The elevator? Ridiculous. A mouse could not run an elevator. Then, quite unexpectedly, a whole plan of action popped into his mind. Ralph had a genuine inspiration.

First he rolled the aspirin to a safe place behind the ashtray stand beside the elevator.

Then, empty-pawed, he climbed the stairs to the second floor and ran down the hall to Room 215, where he squeezed under the door. Keith was still half awake, his eyes glinting with fever under their heavy lids.

"Pst!" said Ralph. "I've found an aspirin for you."

"Hm-m?" murmured Keith.

"An aspirin tablet. I've found an aspirin!"

"Where is it?" Keith was more awake now.

"Down on the first floor."

"Oh." Keith was obviously disappointed.

"Now wait," said Ralph. "I can get it up here, but I've got to have some help. You'll have to let me take your sports car."

"You're too young," mumbled Keith.

"I am *not*." And it was true that Ralph felt very much older than he had when he lost the motorcycle. "Come on. You need that aspirin, don't you?"

"You already lost my motorcycle."

"Oh, come *on*." Ralph was growing more impatient as he felt the night slipping by. "If you won't let me take the sports car, will you let me take the ambulance?"

"I guess so." Keith did not feel equal to arguing with a determined mouse. He picked up his ambulance from the bedside table and set it on the floor. "Here."

"One more thing," said Ralph anxiously. "Do you think you could manage to open the door for me? I know you feel terrible, but it is the last thing I'll ask. Honest. And I promise I'll have the aspirin up here in no time."

Keith sighed but he slid his feet out from under the sheet and, hanging onto the bedside table, reached over and opened the door.

Ralph was already seated in the white ambulance with the red cross painted on the side. "*Wh-e-e. Wh-e-e. Wh-e-e.*" He took the corner into the hall on two wheels and sped down the bare floor between the wall and the carpet until he came to Room 211. Here

he slowed down and then went, "*Wh-e-e!*
Wh-e-e! Wh-e-e!" good and loud. This carried him, as he had planned, to the elevator.
It was a crucial moment. Now he would
find out if his plan was going to work.

The little dog in Room 211 began to
whimper and then to bark just as Ralph had
planned.

In a moment the door opened and the
man stumbled out with the little terrier in
his arms. "Oh, all right," he grumbled. "I'll
walk you. Shut up, will you?"

Ralph waited, his paws tense on the
steering wheel.

The man walked groggily to the closed
elevator door, where he managed, in spite
of the wriggling dog in his arms, to push the
button. Soon the elevator door slid open.

Ralph knew that timing was important. The man entered the elevator. The
dog barked. "*Wh-e-e! Wh-e-e!*" said Ralph

hard enough and fast enough to shoot the ambulance at great speed across the yawning crack between the floor of the hall and the floor of the elevator before the man turned around. As the dog's owner turned, Ralph steered skillfully around his feet and parked the ambulance behind him. The man pressed the button, the doors closed, and the elevator actually began to descend.

"Do you know what you are?" the man sleepily asked the dog. "You are a nuisance, that's what you are. A four-footed, hair-covered nuisance."

The dog ignored his master. "I know you're down there," he yapped to Ralph. "If I could just get down I'd get you!"

Ralph did not answer. He was taking no chances. He waited quietly inside his ambulance until the man had carried the dog out before he drove out of the elevator. He jumped out of the ambulance, opened the rear doors, seized the precious aspirin, and boosted it inside. Slamming the doors, he ran around and jumped into the driver's seat. There was not an instant to lose.

"*Wh-e-e. Wh-e-e.*" The ambulance moved toward the open elevator, but unfortunately by this time Ralph was slightly out of breath. The front wheels of the ambulance caught in the crack between the floor of the lobby and the floor of the elevator. The ambulance was stuck.

Oh, no, thought Ralph. Not now. I can't fail now. "*Wh-e-e. Wh-e-e,*" he managed to gasp. The wheels spun but the ambulance did not move. Ralph jumped out, put his shoulder to the rear of the vehicle, and pushed with all his strength. Nothing happened. In a moment the man would be returning with his dog.

Desperate, Ralph climbed back into the ambulance. He took a breath so deep

he thought his lungs would surely burst.
"*Wh-e-e! Wh-e-e! Wh-e-e!*" He made the
sound hard and fast and high-pitched. The
wheels spun. The ambulance moved, slowly
at first, and then as the tires got a grip on the
floor of the elevator, it shot out of the crack
and across the elevator and hit the rear wall
with a bump. Ralph collapsed over the steering wheel, limp with relief, just as the man
came back through the lobby with his dog.

"I guess some boy lost his toy ambulance," muttered the man, more awake now, as he stepped in and pressed the button.

Toy! thought Ralph indignantly. This ambulance is carrying medical supplies to the sick.

"Boy, my foot!" yapped the terrier. "It's that dastardly mouse. Let me down and I'll get him!"

Ralph did not try to answer. He was saving all his breath now to get the ambulance across that crack once more.

The man slapped the dog lightly on the nose and said, "Be quiet! I took you outside, didn't I?"

Fortunately the elevator door stayed open behind the man as he walked out, so Ralph had no trouble driving the ambulance out and down the hall to Room 215. The door had blown shut but he did not care. He jumped out of the ambulance and ran around to the back, where he unloaded the aspirin, shoved it under the bedroom door, and squeezed under after it.

"Hey, Keith! I've got it!" Ralph was filled with triumph. "I've brought you an aspirin!"

13

A SUBJECT FOR A COMPOSITION

Ralph was a hero in the mousehole that night. His admiring relatives gathered around, begging to hear the story of his adventures. Ralph could not help bragging a little as he told the story of his travels, beginning with the search of the second-floor rooms, skipping the part about the teacher trapping him under a drinking glass, and ending with Keith's taking the

aspirin and finally falling asleep.

"But are you sure it really was an aspirin
tablet?" Ralph's mother could always find
something to worry about. "Are you sure it
wasn't some other kind of pill?"

"Keith put it on the bedside table and
refused to take it until his mother saw it,"
explained Ralph. "At first his mother and
father got pretty excited and thought he
was out of his mind from the fever when he

started telling them there was an aspirin on the table. Then when they saw the pill and could tell from the letters on it that it really was an aspirin they decided the night clerk must have found it and brought it up. They thought the windows rattled so much they did not hear his knock."

"Oh, Ralph, I am so proud of you," said his mother with a sigh of relief while his brothers and sisters and cousins stared at him with shining eyes.

"Good work, Ralph. I didn't think you could do it," said Uncle Lester heartily.

"I feel much better about room service now that we have left an aspirin for a tip," said Ralph's mother. "I feel that at last we have done the right thing."

"Our Ralph is growing up," said Aunt Sissy.

"Yes, Ralph is growing up," agreed his mother with a sad note in her voice. "It's hard to believe. It seems only yesterday that he was a tiny pink mouse without any hair."

Naturally this embarrassed Ralph, but now that his mother had finally admitted he was growing up, he decided to make the most of this moment. "*Now* can I go down to the first floor by myself?" he asked eagerly.

"We'll see," said his mother, looking worried once more.

"Nonsense," said Uncle Lester. "Of course he may go. Ralph has shown that he can be a very responsible mouse."

"I guess you're right," agreed Ralph's mother nervously.

"Oh, boy!" exclaimed Ralph.

"Tell us again how you climbed down the vine and the owl nearly got you," begged a cousin.

"No, tell us again how the ambulance got stuck in the crack," said another.

"No, tell the part about how you got the dog to bark," pleaded a third.

The only flaw in the evening for Ralph was the fact that he had not found the motorcycle on his travels through the hotel.

Keith slept soundly and the next morning, although he still had a temperature, Ralph was pleased to see he was feeling much better.

"Do you hurt anyplace?" Mrs. Gridley asked anxiously, after she had given her son an aspirin brought by the milkman. "Is your throat sore? Does your stomach ache?"

Keith shook his head. "I just feel sort of tired."

"He's going to be all right. He must have picked up a bug someplace," said Mrs. Gridley to her husband. "A day in bed with plenty of fluids and he'll be on his feet again."

Mr. Gridley nodded. "Do you feel like eating any breakfast?" he asked Keith. "We can order something for you from room service."

Keith brightened. "Can I really have something sent up from room service?" he asked, and when his father assured him he could, he slumped back into the pillow. "But I'm not hungry."

"Some orange juice would be good for you," suggested his mother.

"All right," agreed Keith, and then added as if he suddenly had an inspiration, "and bacon and toast and jelly."

"Your appetite seems to have come back in a hurry," remarked Mr. Gridley, as he picked up the telephone and asked to be connected with room service to order, he thought, breakfast for his son.

As soon as the adults had gone, Ralph popped out into the room.

"Hi," said Keith. "Thanks a lot for the aspirin. It really helped."

"That's all right," answered Ralph modestly.

"Where did you find it?" Keith was curious to know.

"Under a dresser down on the first floor."

"The first floor!" Keith could not believe it. "How did you manage to get it up here?"

Once more Ralph told the story of his night's adventure, skipping the part about the drinking glass, but making it sound as if he had narrowly escaped the horny talons of the owl as he traveled down the vine.

"Golly!" Keith was amazed at Ralph's story. "You know what? You're a pretty smart mouse. And a brave one, too."

"It was nothing," said Ralph in an off-hand manner.

"Nothing! It was plenty. You risked your life!"

The boy's admiration and gratitude made Ralph feel even prouder of what he had done. "I parked your ambulance out in the hall," he said, wanting Keith to know how responsible he was. "Your folks will probably see it and bring it in when they come back."

"That reminds me. You didn't happen to see my motorcycle anyplace, did you?" Keith's question was unexpected.

"Well, no, I didn't." Ralph suddenly felt less proud of himself. "But I didn't have much time to look."

"Yeah, I know." Keith was sympathetic. "I just wondered. . . ."

A knock at the door sent Ralph scurrying to the knothole.

"Come in," called Keith.

Matt entered with a tray. "Here you are and here is your ambulance. I found it out in the hall," he said as he set the tray across Keith's knees. "Sorry to see you're under the weather."

"Thank you. I'll be all right." Keith handed Matt a coin his father had left for a

tip. "And thanks for bringing in my ambulance."

Matt pocketed the coin. "Thank you,"
he said, "and, by the way, this doesn't happen to be yours, does it?" He pulled the
little motorcycle out of his pocket.

Ralph was so excited he almost fell out of the knothole.

"Hey!" Keith sat up straight, rocking the orange juice on his tray. "It sure is. Where did you find it?"

"In a hamper of linen that had been chewed by mice. Or by a mouse. It fell out when the housekeeper was showing us the damage that had been done. I picked it up before anyone noticed it."

"Gee, thanks. Thanks a lot." Keith accepted the motorcycle and set it on his tray. "It's my favorite. I didn't like losing it."

"I wonder how it got into that hamper of linen?" mused Matt.

Keith grinned but said nothing.

Old Matt rubbed his chin and stared at the ceiling. "I don't suppose a certain irresponsible mouse happened to ride it into a pile of sheets and pillowcases and get tangled up and dumped into the hamper."

Keith tried not to laugh. "I don't know

171

any irresponsible mice," he said. "Only one responsible mouse. Say, how did you guess?"

"There isn't much around this hotel that escapes my attention," said Matt. "I saw that mouse out in the hall with the little motorcycle. I imagine he's a regular speed demon."

Ralph could no longer stay out of the conversation. "I'm fast but I'm careful. I haven't had an accident yet," he boasted, and added hastily, recalling his fall into the wastebasket, "at least not since I learned to ride the motorcycle."

"If there is anything I can't stand, it's a cheeky mouse," remarked Matt good-naturedly. "What do you call getting tangled up in a lot of linen?"

"What I mean is, I didn't crack up in the motorcycle," said Ralph with dignity.

"He's not cheeky," defended Keith. "He's brave. You—you aren't going to tell the management about him, are you?"

"What's the use?" said Matt. "If they get rid of these mice more will move in. Anyway, he's a cute little fellow. It cheers me up just to think of him tearing around on a little motorcycle."

If only I could, thought Ralph.

There followed an unusually pleasant day for the mice. Keith stuffed the bacon and toast and jelly through the knothole. The mice feasted on bacon and jelly before the ants could get at them and stored the toast against the rapidly approaching time when Keith must leave the hotel. They slept all morning while Keith alternately napped and played with his cars. For lunch they enjoyed peanut butter sandwiches again.

Ralph did not sleep well that afternoon. He found himself thinking of the tantalizing glimpse he had had of the ground floor and of all the opportunities it offered mice—crumbs in the dining room, leftovers in the kitchen, scraps in the garbage. He lay daydreaming on a pile of shredded Kleenex. He could see himself on the first floor pilfering crumbs in the dining room at night after the guests were in bed. And from the dining room he would go to the kitchen right past the night clerk, who was sure to be asleep. If only he could make the trip on the motorcycle. . . .

The thought of the motorcycle put an end to Ralph's daydream and made sleep impossible. After tossing about on his bed of Kleenex, he got up and poked his head out the knothole. Keith was awake, lying back on the pillows with his cars beside him. He smiled wanly at Ralph.

"How are you feeling?" asked Ralph.

"Sort of tired," answered Keith.

Ralph climbed through the hole. "Where are your folks?"

"They went out for a little while. They'll be back. I'm supposed to take a nap."

"Are you going to?" asked Ralph.

"I'd rather talk to you." Keith leaned over and set the motorcycle on the floor. "Want to ride it?" he asked.

"Do I want to ride it!" Ralph could scarcely believe he had heard correctly. "You mean you'll let me? After the way I lost it for you?"

"You proved you could be responsible when you brought me the aspirin," explained Keith. "You're more grown up."

"Thanks," said Ralph modestly.

"I guess mice grow up faster than boys." Keith sounded as though he longed to grow as rapidly as a mouse.

"You grow a little bit every day," Ralph said, as he removed his crash helmet from its hiding place behind the curtain.

"I guess you're right," agreed Keith. "My

dad measures me every six months against the doorjamb of our kitchen back in Ohio, and each mark he makes is higher than the last, but I never feel myself growing."

"You wait long enough and you will be a grown-up." Ralph felt as if he had said something very wise as he slipped the rubber band on his crash helmet around his whiskers.

"I guess so." Keith slumped back on the pillows. "But it takes so long."

"I grew up, didn't I?" asked Ralph. "You said yourself I had become a responsible mouse."

"Yes, you did," said Keith thoughtfully. "I guess that's part of the secret. Just getting bigger isn't enough. You have to learn things like not taking off down a steep hill on a bicycle when you aren't used to hand brakes. Stuff like that."

Ralph walked with a slight swagger to

the motorcycle, grabbed the handgrips, and threw his leg across the seat. He remembered to pick up his tail before he started. *Pb-pb-b-b-b.* He took off across the carpet and circled the room, covering the rough parts under the dresser and chair and coming to a halt beside the bed. "She has good balance on a rough road," said Ralph with authority. "She's a mighty fine machine."

"Say, Ralph," said Keith, suddenly sitting up. "How would you like to come with me when we leave the hotel?"

"Come with you!" Ralph was stunned. He had expected to live and die in the Mountain View Inn, and now he was being offered the opportunity for travel that he had dreamed of.

"Yes. Come with me to San Francisco and then back to Ohio."

Ralph's first thought was of the motorcycle. If he went with Keith he would not have to be separated from the motorcycle.

Keith must have sensed Ralph's thoughts because he said, "You could ride the motorcycle every day."

Ralph was silent. He had begun to think of other things—his family, the permission he had earned to visit the ground floor, Keith's family and how they might feel about a mouse.

"Come on, Ralph," said Keith. "You could travel in my pocket."

"Your mother doesn't care for mice," Ralph pointed out.

"Not running around loose," agreed Keith. "But she let me keep a couple of white mice once. I still have their cage at home. You would be very comfortable in it."

"Comfortable in a cage?" Ralph was horrified. "No, thank you."

"Aw, come on—"

"Would you like to be shut up in a cage?" demanded Ralph.

"Well, no, but—"

"Neither would I," said Ralph. "Especially now that I can finally go to the ground floor."

In his disappointment Keith slumped back on the pillows once more. "I guess I knew you really wouldn't want to come," he said. "I understand."

"I sure will hate to see this motorcycle leave," said Ralph, and added hastily, "and you, too, of course."

The boy and the mouse were silent. Both were thinking of their wishes and their regrets that their wishes could not come true.

Keith rolled over on his side and propped his head up on his fist. "Would you like to keep the motorcycle?" he asked.

"Keep it! Me?"

"Sure," said Keith. "I can save up my allowance and buy another one when we get back to Ohio."

"You really mean it?" Ralph could

scarcely contain his excitement. "Keep it for my very own?"

"Of course."

"How come?" Ralph wanted to know.

"I just like to think of you riding it," said Keith. "You know—if you grew up enough to be trusted with a mouse-sized motorcycle, maybe someday I could earn a big one."

The excitement drained out of Ralph. "I can't. I don't have any place to keep it. It's too big to go through the knothole, and I couldn't hide it behind the curtain forever because I've heard that after Labor Day when there aren't so many tourists they take the curtains down to be cleaned."

"That is a problem," agreed Keith. "There must be someplace in a big hotel like this where you could keep a motorcycle."

Ralph sat on the motorcycle thinking as hard as he could. In the closet? He couldn't get it out when the door was closed. Under the bed? Eventually it would be found.

"How about downstairs?" suggested Keith. "I could carry it down for you before we leave. There must be a good hiding place down there someplace."

"There's that big old clock my ancestor ran up," said Ralph thoughtfully. "Nobody ever cleans under it, but frankly I don't care to have it striking over my head."

Keith thought awhile. "How about that big television set in the lobby?" he asked. "The noise shouldn't bother you because you would only go under it at night when everyone was asleep."

"Yes!" Ralph was excited. "That's a perfect garage. I saw it when I got the aspirin. The legs are just high enough for the motorcycle but not quite high enough for a vacuum cleaner attachment."

"Then it's settled!" said Keith, and then

added rather sternly, Ralph thought, "But first you must ask your mother."

Ralph dismounted and ran to the knothole. He was gone several minutes before he returned to announce in triumph, "She says I can keep the motorcycle if I promise to drive carefully and wear my crash helmet every single time I ride it."

"Swell!" Keith was just as excited as Ralph. "When we check out I'll hide it for you while my folks are busy paying the bill."

"I can't thank you enough." Ralph fastened his crash helmet once more. "I never thought I would have a motorcycle of my very own."

Keith lay back on the pillow and smiled at the mouse mounting the motorcycle. "It will be fun thinking of you riding around that big old lobby when I'm back in Ohio this winter going to school. And when the teacher asks us to write a composition about our summer vacation I can write about meeting a brave mouse named Ralph who rode a little motorcycle. I'll tell about your bringing the aspirin except I'll have to call it a pill because I can't spell *aspirin*. Of course the teacher won't believe it, but she'll probably say I show imagination."

Ralph felt proud to think he was going to be written about in a composition in far-off Ohio. *Pb-pb-b-b-b.* He grabbed his tail, gunned the motor, and took off, heading for the threadbare part of the carpet that made such a good speedway. Round and round he sped, faster and faster until his whiskers blew back and he was filled with the joy of speed. He longed to wave to Keith, but he realized a good driver must keep both paws on the handgrips. He glanced up and noticed that Keith's eyes were closed. The boy had fallen asleep with a smile on his face.

Ralph dragged his heels to brake the motorcycle. Quietly he parked it beside the bed and quietly he removed his crash helmet and hid it behind the curtain. He did not want to disturb the sleeping boy.

Ralph could wait to ride the motorcycle. It was his to keep.

Want more Ralph?

TURN THE PAGE AND ENJOY THESE
SPECIAL FEATURES!

• Discussion Guide •

• "Who Said It?" Activity •

• First two chapters of *The Mouse and the Motorcycle*

with original art by Louis Darling •

DISCUSSION GUIDE

1. *The Mouse and the Motorcycle* begins with the line:
   *Keith, the boy in the rumpled shorts and shirt, did not
   know he was being watched as he entered Room 215
   of the Mountain View Inn.* Since we don't find out
   who is watching Keith until chapter 2, who did
   you think it was?

2. In which ways are Keith and Ralph similar? How
   are they different? Think about their families,
   interests, and age.

3. Because of Ralph's small stature, normal-sized
   objects could pose a potential threat. Imagine you
   were a small mouse—what kind of things would
   scare you? Which would be fun?

4. Do you find Matt the bellboy to be a friend or a
   foe to Ralph and his family? Explain your reason-
   ing.

5. Why do you think Ralph was so excited to
   finally sit on Keith's motorcycle? Describe the
   significance of his first ride.

6. Were you surprised that Ralph, a mouse, and

3

Keith, a human, could understand each other? If you could speak to any animal, which would it be and why?

7. It seems as though Ralph has more fun with Keith's toy motorcycle than Keith is able to. Why do you think that is? Do you think Keith is jealous of Ralph or happy for him? Describe a similar experience you may have had.

8. Ralph's mother warns him of associating with humans—similar to how Keith's mom is afraid of mice. Why do you think one fears the other?

9. When Ralph loses Keith's motorcycle, he dreads having to tell Keith. Share a time that you were afraid of telling someone the truth. What was the outcome?

10. In chapter 9, Keith tells Ralph that he's in a hurry to grow up. Have you ever felt that way? What did you do about it?

11. What does Ralph's risky adventure to find an aspirin tablet say about his friendship with Keith?

12. Over the course of the story, Ralph encounters a number of threatening situations: being trapped

in a wastebasket, getting barked at by a small dog, almost getting vacuumed, and being tossed out the window by Mary Lou and Betty. Which circumstance did you find to be the most dangerous? Why?

13. Why is it so important for Ralph to show his family that he can be brave and responsible?

14. In the beginning of the story, Keith's mom didn't want to stay at the Mountain View Inn, but instead, wanted to keep driving until the family found another hotel. How would the events of Ralph's and Keith's lives have changed had they not met each other?

15. There are two more books in the Ralph Mouse series. Where do you think Ralph's adventurous spirit will take him next?

WHO SAID IT—KEITH OR RALPH?

Ralph and Keith are very different from each other. For starters, one is a human and one is a mouse. But after bonding over their love of motorcycles, Keith and Ralph learn they're not so different from each other after all.

Read the quotes below. Can you guess who said each line?

1. I'm growing up. I want to go out and see the world.
2. Whew! That was close.
3. I bet you like to look at big motorcycles yourself.
4. My mother would never let me ride a motorcycle. She would say I might break a leg or something silly like that.
5. I don't know why people say things are quiet as mice.
6. I'm not too young and I haven't a moment to lose.
7. I guess that's my trouble, too. I don't stop to use my head.
8. You wait long enough and you will be a grown-up.

9. I guess that's part of the secret. Just getting bigger isn't enough. You have to learn things.

10. My motorcycle! Somebody stole my motorcycle!

11. That motorcycle was my very most favorite.

12. The hard part is, I *am* in a hurry. I don't want to do kid things. I want to do big things. Real things.

13. So do I. I want to grow up.

14. It's all right. I've already ordered. Room service is bringing us bacon and toast with jelly.

15. I like that motorcycle and I don't want anything to happen to it.

16. I know what you mean. Thinking about the motorcycle makes me feel awful, too.

17. Don't worry. I won't let you down.

18. I guess mice grow up faster than boys.

19. She's a mighty fine machine.

20. Would you like to be shut up in a cage?

Key: 1: R, 2: K, 3: R, 4: K, 5: K, 6: R, 7: R, 8: R, 9: K, 10: K, 11: K, 12: K, 13: R, 14: R, 15: K, 16: R, 17: K, 18: K, 19: R, 20: R

THE FIRST TWO CHAPTERS OF
THE MOUSE AND THE MOTORCYCLE WITH
ORIGINAL ART BY LOUIS DARLING

Mice come in all shapes and sizes. And Ralph S. Mouse has been drawn many different ways since he was created in 1965. To catch a glimpse of his first rendering, turn the page!

1
THE NEW GUESTS

K eith, the boy in the rumpled shorts and shirt, did not know he was being watched as he entered Room 215 of the Mountain View Inn. Neither did his mother and father, who both looked hot and tired. They had come from Ohio and for five days had driven across plains and deserts and over mountains to the old hotel in the California foothills twenty-five miles from

11

Highway 40.

The fourth person entering Room 215 may have known he was being watched, but he did not care. He was Matt, sixty if he was a day, who at the moment was the bellboy. Matt also replaced worn-out lightbulbs, renewed washers in leaky faucets, carried trays for people who telephoned room service to order food sent to their rooms, and sometimes prevented children from hitting one another with croquet mallets on the lawn behind the hotel.

Now Matt's right shoulder sagged with the weight of one of the bags he was carrying. "Here you are, Mr. Gridley. Rooms 215 and 216," he said, setting the smaller of the bags on a luggage rack at the foot of the double bed before he opened a door into the next room. "I expect you and Mrs. Gridley will want Room 216. It is a corner room with twin beds and a private bath." He carried the heavy bag into the next room, where he could be heard opening windows. Outside a chipmunk chattered in a pine tree and a chickadee whistled *fee-bee-bee*.

The boy's mother looked critically around Room 215 and whispered, "I think we should drive back to the main highway. There must be a motel with a *Vacancy* sign someplace. We didn't look long enough."

"Not another mile," answered the father. "I'm not driving another mile on a California highway on a holiday weekend. Did you see the way that truck almost forced us off the road?"

"Dad, did you see those two fellows on motorcycles—" began the boy and stopped, realizing he should not interrupt an argument.

"But this place is so *old*," protested the boy's mother. "And we have only three weeks for our whole trip. We had planned to spend the Fourth of July weekend in San Francisco and we wanted to show Keith as much of the United States as we could."

"San Francisco will have to wait, and this is part of the United States. Besides, this used to be a very fashionable hotel," said Mr. Gridley. "People came from miles around."

"Fifty years ago," said Mrs. Gridley. "And they came by horse and buggy."

The bellboy returned to Room 215. "The dining room opens at six-thirty, sir. There is Ping-Pong in the game room, TV in the lobby, and croquet on the back lawn. I'm sure you will be very comfortable." Matt, who had seen guests come and go for many years, knew there were two kinds—those who thought the hotel was a dreadful old barn of a place and those who thought it charming and quaint, so quiet and restful.

"Of course we will be comfortable," said Mr. Gridley, dropping some coins into Matt's hand for carrying the bags.

"But this big old hotel is positively spooky." Mrs. Gridley made one last protest. "It is probably full of mice."

Matt opened the window wide. "Mice? Oh no, ma'am. The management wouldn't stand for mice."

"I wouldn't mind a few mice," the boy said, as he looked around the room at the high ceiling, the knotty pine walls, the carpet so threadbare that many of its roses had almost entirely faded, the one chair with the antimacassar on its back, the washbasin and towel racks in the corner of the room. "I like it here," he announced. "A whole room to myself. Usually I just get a cot in the corner of a motel room."

His mother smiled, relenting. Then she turned to Matt. "I'm sorry. It's just that it was so hot crossing Nevada and we are not used to mountain driving. Back on the highway the traffic was bumper to bumper. I'm sure we shall be very comfortable."

After Matt had gone, closing the door behind him, Mr. Gridley said, "I need a rest before dinner. Four hundred miles of driving and that mountain traffic! It was too much.”

“And if we are going to stay for a week-end I had better unpack,” said Mrs. Gridley. “At least I’ll have a chance to do some drip-drying.”

Alone in Room 215 and unaware that he was being watched, the boy began to explore. He got down on his hands and knees and looked under the bed. He leaned out the open window as far as he could and greedily inhaled deep breaths of pine-scented air. He turned the hot and cold water on and off in the washbasin and slipped one of the small bars of paper-wrapped soap into his pocket. Under the window he discovered a knothole

in the pine wall down by the floor and, squatting, poked his finger into the hole. When he felt nothing inside he lost interest.

Next Keith opened his suitcase and took out an apple and several small cars—a sedan, a sports car, and an ambulance about six inches long, and a red motorcycle half the length of the cars—which he dropped on the striped bedspread before he bit into the apple. He ate the apple noisily in big chomping bites, and then laid the core on the bedside table between the lamp and the telephone.

Keith began to play, running his cars up and down the bedspread, pretending that the stripes on the spread were highways and making noises with his mouth—*vroom vroom* for the sports car, *wh-e-e wh-e-e* for the ambulance, and *pb-pb-b-b-b* for the motorcycle, up and down the stripes.

Once Keith stopped suddenly and looked quickly around the room as if he expected to see something or someone, but when he saw nothing unusual he returned to his cars. *Vroom vroom. Bang! Crash!* The sports car hit the sedan and rolled over off the highway stripe. *Pb-pb-b-b-b.* The motorcycle came roaring to the scene of the crash.

"Keith," his mother called from the next room. "Time to get washed for dinner."

"OK." Keith parked his cars in a straight line on the bedside table beside the telephone, where they looked like a row of real cars only much, much smaller.

The first thing Mrs. Gridley noticed when she and Mr. Gridley came into the room was the apple core on the table. She dropped it with a thunk into the metal wastebasket beside the table as she gave several quick little sniffs of the air and said, looking perplexed, "I don't care what the bellboy said. I'm sure this hotel has mice."

"I hope so," muttered Keith.

2
THE MOTORCYCLE

Except for one terrifying moment when the boy had poked his finger through the mousehole, a hungry young mouse named Ralph eagerly watched everything that went on in Room 215. At first he was disappointed at the size of the boy who was to occupy the room. A little child, preferably two or even three children, would have been better. Little messy children were always considerate about leaving crumbs on the carpet. Oh well, at least these people did not have a dog. If there was one thing Ralph disliked, it was a snoopy dog.

Next Ralph felt hopeful. Medium-sized boys could almost always be counted on to leave a sticky candy bar wrapper on the floor or a bag of peanuts on the bedside table, where Ralph could reach them by climbing up the telephone cord. With a boy this size, the food, though not apt to be plentiful, was almost sure to be of good quality.

The third emotion felt by Ralph was joy when the boy laid the apple core by the telephone. This was followed by despair when the mother dropped the core into the metal wastebasket. Ralph knew that anything at the bottom of a metal wastebasket was lost to a mouse forever.

A mouse lives not by crumbs alone and so Ralph experienced still another emotion; this time food was not the cause of it. Ralph was eager, excited, curious, and impatient all at once. The emotion was so strong it made him forget his empty stomach. It was caused by those little cars, especially that motorcycle and the *pb-pb-b-b-b* sound the boy made. That sound seemed to satisfy something within Ralph, as if he had been waiting all his life to hear it.

Pb-pb-b-b-b went the boy. To the mouse the sound spoke of highways and speed, of distance and danger, and whiskers blown back by the wind.

The instant the family left the room to go to dinner, Ralph scurried out of the mousehole and across the threadbare carpet to the telephone cord, which came out of a hole in the floor beside the bedside table.

"Ralph!" scolded his mother from the mousehole. "You stay away from that telephone cord!" Ralph's mother was a great

worrier. She worried because their hotel was old and run-down and because so many rooms were often empty with no careless guests to leave crumbs behind for mice. She worried about the rumor that their hotel was to be torn down when the new highway came through. She worried about her children finding aspirin tablets. Ralph's father had tried to carry an aspirin tablet in his cheek pouch, the aspirin had dissolved with unexpected suddenness, and Ralph's father had been poisoned. Since then no member of the family would think of touching an aspirin tablet, but this did not prevent Ralph's mother from worrying.

Most of all Ralph's mother worried about Ralph. She worried because he was a reckless mouse, who stayed out late in the daytime when he should have been home safe in bed. She worried when Ralph climbed the curtain to sit on the windowsill to watch the chipmunk in the pine tree outside and the cars in the parking lot below. She worried because Ralph wanted to go exploring down the hall instead of traveling under the floorboards like a sensible mouse. Heaven only knew what dangers he might meet in the hall—maids, bellboys, perhaps even cats. Or what was worse, vacuum cleaners. Ralph's mother had a horror of vacuum cleaners.

Ralph, who was used to his mother's worries, got a good running start and was already halfway up the telephone cord.

"Remember your Uncle Victor!" his mother called after him.

Ralph seemed not to hear. He climbed the cord up to the telephone, jumped down, and ran around to the row of cars. There it was on the end—the motorcycle! Ralph stared at it and then walked over and kicked a tire. Close up the motorcycle looked even better than he expected. It was new and shiny and had a good set of tires. Ralph walked all the way around it, examining the pair of chromium mufflers and the engine and the hand clutch. It even had a little license plate so it would be legal to ride it.

"Boy!" said Ralph to himself, his whiskers quivering with excitement. "Boy, oh, boy!" Feeling that this was an important moment in his life, he took hold of the handgrips. They felt good and solid beneath his paws. Yes, this motorcycle was a good machine all right. He could tell by the feel. Ralph threw a leg over the motorcycle and sat jauntily on the plastic seat. He even bounced up and down. The seat was curved just right to fit a mouse.

But how to start the motorcycle? Ralph did not know. And even if he did know how to start it, he could not do much riding up here on the bedside table. He considered pushing the motorcycle off onto the floor, but he did not want to risk damaging such a valuable machine.

Ralph bounced up and down on the seat a couple more times and looked around for some way to start the motorcycle. He pulled at a lever or two but nothing happened. Then a terrible thought spoiled his pleasure. This was only a toy. It would not run at all.

Ralph, who had watched many children in Room 215, had picked up a lot of information about toys. He had seen a boy from Cedar Rapids throw his model airplane on the floor because he could not make its plastic parts fit properly. A little girl had burst into tears and run sobbing to her mother when her doll's arm had come out of its socket. And then there was that nice boy, the potato chip nibbler, who stamped his foot because the batteries kept falling out of his car.

But this toy could not be like all those other toys he had seen. It looked too perfect with its wire spokes in its wheels and its pair of shiny chromium exhaust pipes. It would not be right if it did not run. It would not be *fair*. A motorcycle that looked as real as this one *had* to run. The secret of making it run must be perfectly simple if only Ralph had someone to show him what it was.

Ralph was not satisfied just sitting on the motorcycle. Ralph craved action. After all, what was a motorcycle for if it wasn't action? Who needed motorcycle riding lessons? Not Ralph! He tried pushing himself along with his feet. This was not nearly fast enough, but it was better than nothing. He moved his feet faster along the tabletop and then lifted them up while he coasted. Feeling braver, he bent low over the handlebars and worked his feet still faster toward the edge of the bedside table. When he worked up a little speed he would coast around the corner. He scrabbled his feet on the tabletop to gain momentum. In a split second he would steer to the left—

At that moment the bell on the telephone rang half a ring, so close that it seemed to pierce the middle of Ralph's bones. It rang just that half ring, as if the girl at the switchboard realized she had rung the wrong room and had jerked out the cord before the ring was finished.

That half a ring was enough. It shattered Ralph's nerves and terrified him so that he forgot all about steering. It jumbled his thoughts until he forgot to drag his heels for brakes. He was so terrified he let go of the handgrips. The momentum of the motorcycle carried him forward, over the edge of the table. Down, down through space tumbled Ralph with the motorcycle. He tried to straighten out, to turn the fall into a leap, but the motorcycle got in his way. He grabbed in vain at the air with both paws. There was nothing to clutch, nothing to save him, only the empty air. For a fleeting instant he thought of his poor old Uncle Victor. That was the instant the motorcycle landed with a crash in the metal wastebasket.

Ralph fell in a heap beside the motorcycle and lay still.

More great Harper Classics!

Katherine Paterson

E. B. White
PICTURES BY GARTH WILLIAMS

Neil Gaiman
WITH ILLUSTRATIONS BY DAVE McKEAN

Thanhhà Lại

C. S. Lewis

Beverly Cleary

Katherine Applegate

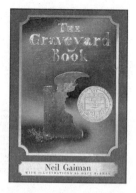

Sharon Creech